TREASURY OF
MAGICAL TALES
FROM AROUND THE WORLD

DONNA JO NAPOLI

★

ILLUSTRATIONS BY **CHRISTINA BALIT**

WASHINGTON, D.C.

Table of Contents

Introduction

This is a collection of tales from around the globe tied together by the thread of magic. All have their origins in oral storytelling—that is, storytelling through voice and gestures, including poems and chants and songs. Many scholars of cultural evolution believe that human beings have been telling stories around evening campfires or in the dark of night for tens of thousands of years. Storytelling can fill time that might otherwise feel lonely or frightening.

Unlike myths, the magical stories offered here are rarely meant to praise gods or otherworldly spirits. They are not minding a religious code. They do not aim to tell you how best to live your life. And they usually do not try to explain natural phenomena. They are grounded in the traditions of their time and place, yes, but in a way distinct from many other kinds of traditional tales. Often when we speak of traditions, we intend religion, language, music, food, clothing, housing … things we can easily point to and identify and things that are often tightly bound to a specific place and time. Traditions in these tales, however, include the hopes and fears of generations—ephemeral things that defy easy definition and that belong more to our common humanity than to any particular culture. In a sense, then, magical tales give us a record of the history of the human spirit.

I often retell traditional tales that are myths or religious stories, and when I do, I tend to stay as close to the original details and tone of the story as I know how to do. In the present volume, however, I stray from that because I want to keep the focus on how the stories here deal with hopes and fears—a tradition that can belong to any place and any time. So as I wrote this volume, I kept in mind the modern sensibility and tried to bring stories from far away and long ago to today's children in a way that can ring true as we look around our own worlds. It was a delightful challenge.

Stories of this sort make us laugh, cry, shiver, grow angry … sometimes with respect to our own foibles and confusions. These tales confront us with aspects of our local world that we might not easily discuss or might even be prohibited from discussing. Moments of injustice are common, as are experiences of sudden loss. Longings for an easy life of luxury can form an undercurrent.

Sitting in a group around a storyteller who brings up these sticky topics can give us comfort. The silly things the characters do offer us relief from the burden of always trying to be responsible in our own lives. The chances characters take can embolden us in making choices. The lessons characters learn—which can be harsh—can give us a safe way of considering possible results if we were to act rashly ourselves. But most of all, seeing characters who dream and cringe like we do reminds us that those around us are just like us in this way. Storytelling binds a community as much as working together for common goals does.

Oral traditional stories can lose some of their charm and power when they appear in written form. The tendency in many oral traditions is to repeat, but repetition in text gets annoying. Plus, in oral traditions the storyteller and audience can interact, where the reactions of one can affect the other. So I urge you to share these stories aloud with someone. Ham it up. Play with tone and body postures and hand gestures. The tales here were selected to make you smile and laugh. I hope you enjoy reading them as much as I enjoyed writing them.

ITALY

The Speaking Bird

 poor man made his living selling wild herbs gathered from forests and along city walls. His three daughters made their living spinning and selling yarn from wool caught on bushes as sheep passed on their way to meadow. When the father died, the three sisters became even poorer.

The king of their city was a worried sort. At night he lurked in the shadows outside houses, eavesdropping. He wanted to know what his subjects said about him. One night he overheard the sisters.

The oldest sister said, "If I were the wife of the royal butler, I'd make sure everyone had plenty to drink. I'd fill one glass and they'd pass it around, and it would never empty."

The middle sister said, "If I were the wife of the keeper of the royal wardrobe, I'd clothe everyone, all with a single piece of cloth that would never run out."

The youngest sister said, "If I were the king's wife, we would have triplets. Two sons born with apples in their hands, and a daughter born with a star on her forehead."

The next morning the king had his servants bring those sisters to him. He handed the oldest girl a glass of water and said, "Prove your words from last night."

The oldest sister carried the glass from one royal attendant to the next. All drank, yet the glass still held water. The oldest sister was as astonished as everyone else; after all, the sisters' talk had been but idle dreams. But the king was satisfied. "You are now the wife of the royal butler."

The king handed a piece of cloth and a pair of scissors to the middle sister. "Prove your words from last night." The middle sister cut clothing for all the royal attendants, and still there was cloth left. The middle sister was astonished. Again, though, the king was satisfied.

"You are now the wife of the keeper of the royal wardrobe."

The king turned to the youngest sister. "I will give you a chance to prove your words. You will be my queen. If you bear me the triplets you described last night, for the rest of your life you will want for nothing. But if you fail, woe to you."

The youngest sister blinked in fear. But her older sisters had been lucky. So she let herself hope. She became queen.

The older sisters, while they were no longer poor, were servants. They grew envious of the youngest sister. They hated her.

The youngest sister soon became pregnant. Not long before she gave birth, the king declared war on another kingdom. He told his servants that if his queen gave birth to triplets, two boys with apples in their hands and a girl with a star on her forehead, all would be well. But if not, they were to send word to him. And he rode off to battle.

The youngest sister gave birth to triplets exactly as she had foretold. She kissed each with gratitude and wonder. But her envious sisters bribed the nursemaid to get rid of the babies and put puppies in their

place. Word was sent to the king that his queen had produced three puppies. In a rage, the king sentenced her to run inside the treadmill that worked the crane used for building the new cathedral.

The nursemaid took the three babies outside the city walls and left them for wild beasts to devour. But three fairies happened by.

"What darling children! Let's give them presents. I give them a deer as nursemaid."

"I give them a purse that never runs out of money."

"I give them a ring that will change color whenever misfortune comes to any one of them."

And so a deer raised the children. Once they were grown, the first fairy returned. "Here are suitable clothes. Go rent a house in the city across from the palace."

The three young people moved to the city, and the purse that never ran out of money served them well; they furnished their home like a palace.

The children's aunts, who still worked at the king's palace, soon noticed them. In horror, they questioned the old nursemaid. "What did you do? Our nephews and niece are alive! See the apples in their hands! See the star on her forehead! Alas, the trouble you've made."

"Don't worry," the nursemaid said to the aunts. "I'll handle this." One day, when the two brothers had gone out, the nursemaid introduced herself to the girl. "You have lovely things," she said. "But you need something that will make you truly happy." She leaned close. "The Dancing Water. Your brothers will get it for you … if they love you."

When one of the brothers came home, the sister said, "If you love me, you'll get me the Dancing Water."

This brother didn't know what the Dancing Water was. But he loved his sister. So he set out to find it.

He met a hermit who asked him, "Where are you going, horseman?"

"To fetch the Dancing Water."

"What?! You're going to your death. But stay on the journey until you meet a hermit older than me."

The brother cringed. Still, his love for his sister was boundless. So he continued on until he met a second, older hermit. That hermit gave him the same instructions. The brother quivered, but he continued on. He met a third hermit, so old that his white beard hung down to his feet.

This hermit said, "Climb that mountain. On top is a house with a beautiful gate. Four giant swordsmen guard the gate. Pay attention now. When the giants' eyes are closed, do not enter. But when their eyes open, enter. You'll come to a door. If it is open, do not enter. If it is closed, open it and enter. Four lions will sit there. If their eyes are closed, do not pass by them. If their eyes are open, go past. That's where the Dancing Water is."

Back home, the sister twisted the magic ring on her finger. It stayed green, so she knew her brother was still safe.

It took days for the brother to climb the mountain. The giants stood before the gate with closed eyes. So the brother waited. When their eyes opened, he went through the gate. The door ahead of him stood open. So the brother waited. When it closed, he opened it and went inside. The four lions before him had closed eyes. So the brother waited. When their eyes opened, he passed by them. There was the Dancing Water! He filled many bottles with it. Then, when the lions' eyes were open, he escaped.

Meanwhile, back in the city, the aunts were happy. Surely the nephew who had gone to find the Dancing Water was dead.

But what was this? The nephew returned!

The aunts had two golden basins made, and they had the nursemaid sneak into the young people's home and set those basins side by side. Then the aunts huddled outside the window. The nephew poured water into one basin. It leaped from that basin to the other and back

again. The Dancing Water! The aunts scolded the old
nursemaid, "Your fault, your fault!"

Once again, the nursemaid visited the sister when she was alone.
"The Dancing Water is beautiful. But it can't compare to the Singing
Apple. That will make you supremely happy. Your brothers will get it
for you … if they love you."

The sister asked the same brother to bring her the Singing Apple.
Once more he passed by hermits who gave him instructions. He
arrived at the mountaintop, and made it past the giant swordsmen
and the door that kept opening and closing and the lions. He came
to a pair of garden shears. They were closed. So he waited. When the
shears opened, he went past them and saw a tree with an apple on top.
He climbed the tree, snatched that apple, and rode home.

Meanwhile, the aunts laughed, for surely that nephew couldn't have
been lucky enough to survive the journey twice. But then he reappeared
with the Singing Apple! The aunts ran for the old nursemaid, who then

ran for the sister. This time the nursemaid told the girl that to become wildly happy, she needed the Speaking Bird.

The same brother went off in search of the Speaking Bird. He met hermits, climbed the mountain, passed the giant swordsmen and the opening and closing door and the four lions. He entered a garden with statues and a fountain, in the midst of which was a basin where the Speaking Bird perched.

The bird squawked. "Ridiculous one! Your aunts sent you to your death. You'll be no better off than your mother, who works the treadmill."

His mother? The brother had been instructed not to speak to the bird, but only to pluck a wing feather, dip it in a jar of oil, and anoint the statues with it. But he couldn't stop himself from asking, "Where is my mother?" With those words, the brother became a statue.

Back home, the sister's ring changed color to blue. "Help," said the sister to her other brother. "Go save our brother."

The second brother met the same three hermits, climbed the mountain, and got past all the obstacles. At last, he stood in the garden beside the Speaking Bird. "Absurd one!" said the Speaking Bird. "Now you'll be no better off than your mother, who works the treadmill."

"My mother?" burst out the second brother. And he turned into a statue.

Back home, the sister's ring changed color to black. Wretched world! She went out to find her brothers. She followed the hermits' instructions and arrived at the garden, where the Speaking Bird said to her, "Ridiculous, absurd, obtuse—that's who you three are. Your brothers are statues. Your father is at war. Your mother works the treadmill. Your aunts have won!"

The Speaking Bird flew down and the sister, who wasn't at all obtuse, caught that bird. She plucked a feather from its wing, dipped it in the jar, and anointed her brothers' nostrils. The brothers came to life. The sister anointed all the other statues, who came to life and rejoiced. They were noblemen and princes, barons and kings—all bewitched before but free now.

The sister and brothers returned home and set the Speaking Bird on a perch before the window.

When the king came back from his latest war, he noted the fine home across the street and the young people who lived there. He looked closer. The young men had apples in their hands! The young woman had a star on her forehead! He stood outside the window of that intriguing house. He saw the Dancing Water leap from basin to basin. He swayed to the tune of the Singing Apple.

"What do you think of it all?" the Speaking Bird asked.

The king gasped. This bird had just spoken to him. But he tried to act calm. "It's marvelous."

"Come to dinner on Sunday."

On Sunday the Speaking Bird prepared a feast. The king clapped his hands and said to the young people, "You seem like the children I was supposed to have."

The next Sunday the sister and her brothers and the Speaking Bird went to the king's palace for dinner. The king cozied up to the bird. "Speak to me."

The Speaking Bird said, "These are your children. Your true queen suffers in the treadmill."

The king rushed to his true queen. "Forgive me, please." He folded her into his arms. His arms were better than the treadmill, so the queen agreed. And the children had parents, at last.

What happened to the old nursemaid and the aunts? The king left their fate to the Speaking Bird. He had his children and his true queen, so he didn't care about much else.

BIRD COMMUNICATION

Water doesn't dance and apples don't sing, but some birds do talk. Parrots, especially, have been trained to say words of human languages. Scientists don't know if the parrots actually understand any of the words, however. But birds certainly communicate with each other acoustically via songs, calls, chirps, squawks, whistles, and honks. Many bird species have special songs that seem to carry general messages, such as readiness for breeding or warning to get out of one's territory. The songs of some birds that look the same can differ so much that they don't seem to recognize each other. Some scholars argue that the difference in song "dialects" is enough to classify these birds as belonging to different species.

ENGLAND

Dick Whittington's Cat

ick Whittington was not a lucky child. He had no parents nor even a memory of them. As far as he knew, he had always been alone. He lived in a small village and easily found places to sleep at night—under a bush or a turned-over rowboat by the river, or inside a chicken coop.

Clothes were easy to find, too: Mothers gave him clothes their children had outgrown. But food—that was the problem. The child was always hungry.

One day a man dressed in fancy clothing—a dandy—passed through town. Everyone talked about how rich he was. He had fat red cheeks and a bulging belly. Dick Whittington was sure this man had never been hungry.

"How did that man get so rich?" Dick asked people.

"He's from London."

"Everyone's rich in London."

"The streets are paved with gold."

Gold could buy food. Dick Whittington needed food. So he set off down the road. Soon enough a wagon came bumping along. The friendly driver gave Dick a lift to London town.

And what a town it was! Huge buildings that pierced the sky. People and horses and carriages, clattering by on all sides. And lots of mud in the streets. But no gold.

Dick dropped onto a doorstep and rubbed his eyes.

A woman poked at him with a broom. "Away with you, ragamuffin!"

A man came along the road right then. "Just one minute, Cook," he said. "Let's show a little kindness." The man was the master of that house, so the cook stepped back and Dick entered with the master.

Life got better in one big way: Dick worked in the kitchen, so hunger became a memory. But other things were hard. The cook didn't like him; she smacked him with the broom when no one was watching.

And while Dick now had a room to sleep in, it was overrun with rats and mice that danced on his face at night.

Well, Dick knew how to deal with that. As soon as he'd earned a few pennies, he ran to the ratcatcher and bought one of his cats.

"This is my best one," said the ratcatcher with a wink.

Maybe she was his best and maybe she wasn't. But she was scrappy and strong and ate those rodents snicker-snack. Plus, after eating, she curled up on Dick's chest and purred.

It turned out the master of the house ran a merchant ship. He asked the members of his household if they wanted him to take anything of theirs to sell abroad so they could get some extra money.

The only thing of value Dick had was his cat. And he loved that cat. But he'd come to London to make his fortune, so he put the cat in the merchant's hands.

While the merchant was away on his voyage, the cook was meaner than ever to Dick, the rodent population replenished itself, and Dick couldn't sleep at night without his beloved cat on his chest. Dick was so miserable, he decided to run away. But as he walked along the street, the church bells rang out with a message:

Bong. Dick Whittington, hater of mice.

Bong. Lord Mayor of London you will be.

Bong. Not once, not twice, but thrice.

RAT TROUBLE
Dick Whittington was a real Lord Mayor of London in the Middle Ages, though whether he had a cat is unknown. But in his times, rats were a serious problem in London. Because of the slaughterhouses and the trash on the streets, rats were abundant. In a single year, one rat mother can have 15,000 descendants. And since rats carry fleas that can carry dangerous bacteria, scientists believe that hordes of rats may have been responsible for the nearly 40 outbreaks of the bubonic plague in London from 1348 to 1665.

What? Were the church bells really talking? Lord Mayor? And three times over! Dick rubbed his ears. He better stay in London. He returned to the merchant's house.

Meanwhile, the merchant arrived in a distant land. He was invited to a banquet with the king and queen. But the instant the feast was on the table, rats poured out from everywhere. It was like some terrible evil—a scourge upon the land. The rats demolished the feast.

"Yuck!" said the king. "I hate these rats. They never let me eat in peace."

The baffled merchant stared. Then he smiled. "I have exactly what you need." He produced Dick Whittington's cat, who pounced on the rats with glee.

Another banquet was prepared, and everyone ate in peace while Dick Whittington's cat chewed on rat after rat. Then she hopped onto the queen's lap and purred. The queen laughed.

In payment for the cat, the king and queen gave the merchant a ship full of gold.

The merchant returned to London and, honest soul that he was, he gave that gold to Dick Whittington.

Now, Dick had seen the underside of poverty and he didn't much like it. So he used his money to help the people of London, rich and poor alike. He built a hospital and a church. He cleaned out the ditches in the poorest neighborhoods. He even built a much needed public bathroom. The people of London loved him and elected him Lord Mayor three times.

As for Dick Whittington's cat, well, she was treated like royalty for the rest of her life.

So whatever your starting point might be, your ending point is unknown. You might become Lord Mayor of London, or perhaps a royal ratter.

The Poor Boy and the Golden Lamb

poor man had a son who was growing husky and strong, eating more and more food every day. The man loved his son dearly, but how on earth could he afford to keep feeding him? With tears in his eyes, the man sent the boy out into the world to make a living.

The son searched for work. Since everyone close by was as poor as his father, he had to travel far. But at last he found a man who owned many sheep and was ready to take him on as a shepherd if he could prove he was good at the job.

The boy had a flute that he had carved himself from peach wood. He played that flute as he drove the sheep from one pasture to another, always in search of sweet green grasses. The music kept him company.

The sheep seemed happy enough with this arrangement. But one little lamb, with golden fleece, was happier than the others. The flock trotted along, but oh, this special lamb gamboled and twirled in time to the music. The boy laughed in delight. The golden lamb was a superb companion during what otherwise would have been starkly lonely hours. The boy played his flute, the lamb danced and leapt about, and the hours flashed by like minutes.

The sheep owner watched the boy coming home at the end of the long day surrounded by the flock. He was pleased to see that those sheep looked contented and—could it be?— a little fatter than they had been that morning. And the boy marched along with energy. Clearly, this work suited him. What a find!

"I'd like you to tend my sheep for a whole year," said the sheep owner. "How much pay would you ask for that?"

"I don't want pay, sir. I want that lamb." The boy pointed to the lamb with the golden fleece. His new friend.

A lamb was substantial pay. On the other hand, this boy was a fine worker and having a happy, fat flock was worth it. The sheep owner agreed with a smile.

After the boy had worked a year, the sheep owner gave him the lamb as his wages, and the boy and lamb set off for the boy's old home. That night they stopped at a farmhouse for lodging. The farmer's daughter took one look at the golden lamb and decided that was the most darling animal she'd ever laid eyes on. She determined to steal the lamb. At midnight, she snuck into the barn where the boy and lamb slept. She reached for the lamb, but the instant her hand touched that golden fleece, it stuck fast.

The boy awoke and blinked at the strange situation. But what could he do about it? He fell back asleep.

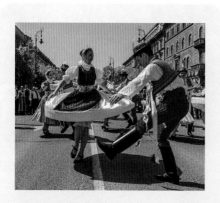

DANCE MOVES

Hungary is famous for its folk music and dance. In many other countries, folk dance is highly regimented. But in Hungary, the tradition is to be creative and improvise, and shepherds' dances are among the most lively, with lots of jumping. Typical instruments are wooden flutes and whistles, horns, bagpipes, and various string instruments. Typical dance moves are turning, crouching, and, in couples dances, the man lifting up the woman and tossing her aside, as though he's "throwing her away."

In the morning, the boy and the lamb continued their journey with the farm girl attached to the lamb's fleece. The boy played his flute as he walked, naturally; the lamb danced and leapt, naturally; and the farm girl had no choice but to dance and leap as well.

A baker saw them, and in annoyance she shouted at the farm girl, "Stop that foolish behavior." The farm girl couldn't stop, but the baker didn't know that. In a fit of pique, the baker picked up her wooden peel for sliding bread in and out of the oven and conked the farm girl on the back. "I told you to stop!" But the farm girl didn't stop. And now the baker's peel was stuck to the farm girl, and the baker was stuck to the peel. As they went down the road, the lamb, the farm girl, and the baker all danced and leapt to the boy's flute music.

A priest coming out of church saw them. "What a spectacle you make! Act right!" But the farm girl and the baker didn't act how the priest wanted them to act; they couldn't. The priest, who was as quick to anger as the baker, smacked the baker on her head with his cane. Of course, the cane stuck, and the priest stuck to the cane. The boy played his flute and continued on while the lamb danced and leapt, the farm girl danced and leapt, the baker danced and leapt, and the priest danced and leapt.

That night the boy and his entourage stopped for lodging at an old woman's cottage. The woman was so relieved to have someone to talk to that she told the boy and the lamb and the farm girl and the baker and the priest all the latest news. The most important news was the plight of the king's daughter. The poor princess was ill and the royal doctors said only laughter could cure her. But no one could even make her smile, much less laugh. The king had made a proclamation: Whoever could make the princess laugh could wed her and become royal himself. The princess agreed. After all, she didn't want to die, and if someone could make her laugh at this point, well, surely, he'd be a fine person to share the rest of her life with.

The boy was eager to try, as was his lamb friend. In the morning they went to the castle and presented themselves for the challenge. The king and the princess stood there, kind, but doubtful—who was this boy with his motley group of friends?

The boy played his flute. The golden lamb danced and leapt; the farm girl and the baker and the priest danced and leapt.

How absurd! The princess gaped. Then she howled with laughter.

The startled lamb shook himself hard, and the farm girl, the baker, and the priest flew through the air, free at last. They all danced for joy now.

The boy married the princess, who was quite happy to have the lamb with the golden fleece be their companion. The farm girl became lady-in-waiting to the princess. The baker became Court Baker. And the priest became Court Chaplain. Once the boy's father heard about all this, he came to the castle to retire.

For a whole week the entire country celebrated the wedding. How? Dancing and leaping, of course.

BERBER, MOROCCO

Half-a-Rooster

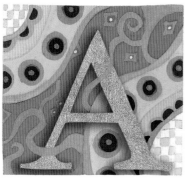

man had two wives who bickered about everything. One wife was wise and one wife was foolish—which might have been the cause of their quarrels.

One day they argued about who owned the rooster. So they cut it in half. The foolish wife cooked her half and ate it. The wise woman let her half live, though she knew the creature would have trouble managing with just one leg, one wing, and half a head.

Half-a-Rooster might have had only half a head, but it was his head, nevertheless, with his thoughts. He decided to leave this home that had turned so horrible and find out what the world could offer.

He set out at dawn. Traveling on just one foot was tiring, so at midday he rested by a brook. A jackal came to the brook for a drink. Half-a-Rooster got a wild idea. He pulled a hair from the jackal's back and hid it under his wing.

Half-a-Rooster continued his journey until nightfall, then he stopped at a tree to sleep. A lion passed. Fast as he could, Half-a-Rooster yanked a hair from the lion and tucked it away with the jackal's hair.

The next day, Half-a-Rooster sauntered along through the forest until midday, when he met a boar. Unlike the jackal and the lion, this boar was alert and noticed Half-a-Rooster

immediately; there was no way to pluck a hair secretly. Half-a-Rooster ruffled the feathers on his half chest and crowed: "The trickiest of animals, the jackal, gave me a hair. The most noble of animals, the lion, gave me a hair." Now, neither of those statements was quite true, but Half-a-Rooster didn't worry about that. "If you want to be in good company, give me a hair, too." The boar wanted to be in good company; he gave Half-a-Rooster a hair.

With the three hairs safe under his wing, Half-a-Rooster was ready to carry out another wild idea. He arrived at the palace of a king. "Listen to me!" His screech was so loud that everyone turned to look. "Tomorrow, the king will die." Everyone gasped. "But the queen needn't worry, for I'll take her as my wife."

What a preposterous and insulting announcement! The king had Half-a-Rooster seized and thrown into the sheep-and-goat pen to be trampled to death.

But Half-a-Rooster hopped to the side of the pen, where a fire was burning. He dangled the tip of the jackal hair into the fire. The jackal came running. "What are you doing? That's my hair!"

"Get rid of these sheep and goats," said Half-a-Rooster.

The jackal gave a yell and a yap and a growl and a howl. His brother jackals appeared at the summons. "Kill those sheep and goats, so Half-a-Rooster will save my hair from the fire." Well,

the jackals made short shrift of the task, the first jackal got his hair back, only a little singed, and Half-a-Rooster scampered off to safety.

The next day the king found the sheep-and-goat pen empty. That absurd rooster was nowhere to be found. But at the midday meal hour, the king heard a loud crowing. "Today is the day! The king will die! And I will marry his queen!" It was that maddening rooster again. The king had him seized and thrown into the cattle yard to be trampled to death for sure this time.

Of course, there was a firepit in the cattle yard, too. Half-a-Rooster dangled the tip of the lion's hair into the fire this time. In seconds, the lion barreled into the yard. "My hair, my hair! What are you doing!"

"Get rid of these cattle," said Half-a-Rooster.

The lion gave a roar that echoed in the heavens. His brother lions appeared at the summons. "Kill those cattle, so Half-a-Rooster will save my hair from the fire." So the lions killed the cattle, the first lion got his hair back, only a little singed, and Half-a-Rooster vanished to a safe spot.

The king raced out to the cattle yard, since no one could ignore that roar, and found it empty. Again that putrid rooster was missing. The king stomped back inside the palace to fret.

At sunset, Half-a-Rooster repeated his announcement: "Doom for the king! Celebration for me and my queen!"

"Seize that nonsensical bird!" screamed the king. "Lock him in a room. I'll strangle him myself."

The king's servants threw Half-a-Rooster into the treasure room. Why they chose that room, no one knows. But Half-a-Rooster took one look at the gold everywhere and realized he didn't really want to marry the queen. He'd never even met her, after all. And he didn't give one hoot whether the king lived or died. What he really wanted was to have his old home back, with the wise wife, but without that hideous foolish wife who had eaten his other half. Maybe this gold could help.

Half-a-Rooster lit a fire and dangled the boar's hair into it.

Suddenly, he heard a loud crash. The boar smashed through a wall of the treasure room. Rocks flew everywhere. "Don't burn my hair!"

"I won't, if you'll get me out of here. The king plans to kill me."

"Go out through the hole I just made in the wall," said the boar.

"But a rock could fall and flatten me."

"All right. I'll get you out another way," said the boar. "But you better take some gold with you."

"My plan exactly."

Half-a-Rooster rolled in the gold until it stuck to him everywhere. Then he swallowed as much of it as his innards could hold. The boar burst through the door of the treasure room and Half-a-Rooster hopped out right behind him.

Half-a-Rooster took the long path home. When he was finally at the cottage, he crawled under a mat and called out, "Mistress, come beat me. Don't be afraid you'll kill me. Just beat hard."

What the wise wife made of these words is hard to tell. But for some reason, she did as the mysterious voice ordered.

"Stop!" crowed Half-a-Rooster. "Now turn over this mat."

The wise wife flipped the mat. There was her rooster—or her half of him. And the ground beneath him sparkled with gold. She welcomed Half-a-Rooster home again—onto her side of the home.

As for the foolish wife, she had nothing but her nasty dog to spend time with, for Half-a-Rooster never even deigned to look upon her with his one eye.

CHICKEN VERSUS DOG

If you cut a rooster in half, it would die. But this fantastical half-a-rooster not only lives, he is smart and thrives. At the end of this story, the wise wife's wily and beloved pet, a chicken, is contrasted to the foolish wife's nasty pet, a dog. This story comes from Morocco, a country that is mostly Muslim. Perhaps this story reflects the fact that chickens in rural communities traditionally had the run of the house and the yard, unlike other livestock, and that in Muslim societies dogs were often considered unclean. So these two animals make a nice contrast to parallel the wise and foolish wives.

ANGOLA

The Frog Who Tried Hard

imana had never met the Sky Maiden, but somehow he decided he wanted to marry her. He wrote a letter to the Sky Maiden's father, the Sun Chief, asking for her hand in marriage. Since he had no idea how to deliver the letter, he went looking for someone else to deliver it.

Kimana said to Rabbit, "Will you deliver this letter for me?"

"What?" said Rabbit. "I can't hop to Heaven."

Kimana said to Antelope, "Will you deliver this letter for me?"

"Are you kidding?" said Antelope. "I can't run to Heaven."

Kimana said to Hawk, "Will you deliver this letter for me?"

"You must be out of your mind," said Hawk. "I can't fly to Heaven."

Now, Frog had been watching Kimana throughout his search. He asked Kimana, "Why not deliver it yourself?"

"I can't," said Kimana.

"Then I will," said Frog.

Kimana laughed. "If Rabbit can't hop there and Antelope can't run there and Hawk can't fly there, how do you think you'll get there?"

"I'll try hard," said Frog.

So Kimana gave the letter to Frog and Frog took it to his home, near a well that the Sun Chief's servants visited daily. Those servants always climbed down from Heaven on Spider's web, filled their water jugs, and climbed back up. Frog tucked the letter safe in his mouth and hid inside the well. When a servant lowered her pitcher into the well, Frog jumped in, then rode up to Heaven inside that pitcher.

As soon as the servants left their pitchers on the floor and went away, Frog jumped out. He spit the letter onto a bench and hid.

The Sun Chief came for water. "What's this? A letter." He read it. Then he went to the servants. "Who brought this letter?"

"Not us."

He read the letter to his wife, the Moon Lady. "What should we do about this Kimana fellow who wants to marry our daughter?"

"Why are you asking me? Ask our daughter."

The Sun Chief asked his daughter if she wanted to marry Kimana.

The daughter cocked her head in thought. "Can he bring a nice wedding gift?"

The Sun Chief wrote a letter and left it on the bench. When the coast was clear, Frog came out and tucked this new letter safely into his mouth. Then he hid in an empty water pitcher.

The next day the servants carried the pitchers down to the well again to fetch more water. Frog jumped out and gave the letter to Kimana.

Kimana read, "If you bring a lot of money, you can marry my daughter." He moaned and groaned. "I can't get to Heaven, so I can't bring the Sun Chief money."

"Then I'll carry it," said Frog.

"A purse of money is heavy," said Kimana. "How will you do it?"

"I'll try hard," said Frog.

Just like before, Frog jumped into a servant's pitcher as she was fetching water. He carried Kimana's money purse in his mouth all the way up to Heaven, then set the purse on the bench and hid.

The Sun Chief found the purse. "What's this?" he said to his servants. "Who brought this purse?"

"Not us."

The Sun Chief asked his wife if the money in the purse was enough.

"Again you're asking me? Ask our daughter."

The Sun Chief asked his daughter.

"Can he come fetch me?"

So the Sun Chief wrote a letter and left it on the bench. And Frog delivered it to Kimana the usual way.

Kimana moaned and groaned. "I can't get to Heaven, so I can't fetch the Sky Maiden."

"Then I'll fetch her," said Frog.

"A bride? You'll fetch a bride?" said Kimana. "How will you do it?"

"I'll try hard," said Frog.

So Frog went back to Heaven one more time, the usual way. When he was alone with the pitchers of water, he spit into each one: *ptui, ptui, ptui.* Then he hid in a remaining empty pitcher.

Everyone drank the water, and everyone got sick.

The Sun Chief called the spirit doctor. The doctor said, "That human who wants to marry your daughter sent the sickness in the form of a frog, who is an evil spirit. It's all because your daughter hasn't gone down to earth to him."

So the Sun Chief asked his wife, who, naturally, told him to ask his daughter, who answered, "All right, I'll go!"

The next day the Sky Maiden went with the servants down Spider's web to the well. Frog jumped out of his pitcher and said, "I'll lead you to your husband."

The Sky Maiden laughed. "How can you do that? You're just a frog."

"I carried a letter to Heaven and a purse full of money. I fetched a bride from Heaven. I can do anything, so long as I try hard."

"Well, that's my sort of fellow," said the Sky Maiden. "I'll marry you."

So the Sky Maiden took Frog back to Heaven and married him. They're still happy. And Kimana is still waiting for his bride.

STRONG AS SILK
Here the Sun Chief's servants climb down a spiderweb with empty pitchers and then climb back up it again with pitchers full of water. That web had to be mighty to hold all that weight. In fact, the silk that is used for a spiderweb's outer rim and spokes—called dragline silk—is mighty. Dragline silk's tensile strength—its resistance to breaking under tension—is only a little less than that of steel, regardless of the size or type of spider. Scientists study the way spider silk is bundled together as they search for design strategies for making new superstrong fibers.

JINDWI, ZIMBABWE

The Old Woman

ong ago there lived an old woman who had four daughters and four sons plus their two dogs. One day the woman went looking for a new place to live.

She wandered until she met a chief. After exchanging greetings, the old woman said, "I seek a place to live in exchange for work."

The chief's advisers told him, "Look at her knee. It's swollen. What kind of work could she possibly do?"

"It's true my knee is damaged. I need this staff to walk. But you can't find a better worker than me."

The chief hesitated. His advisers shook their heads. "Not today," said the chief.

The old woman walked for many days, meeting many chiefs, all of whom looked at her knee and sent her on her way again.

Finally, the old woman came to a chief who had a very large household, comprised of many homes. His advisers pointed out her knee to him, but this chief suspected that the old woman still had useful days left. "I will ask my queens if they can use your services in exchange for shelter."

The first queen said, "I have a passel of children. What would I do with an old woman who needs to use a staff just to walk around?"

The second queen said, "Even if she could help, I have no food to spare."

And so it went, all down the line of queens, to the very last, who was not much in the chief's favor. In fact, we could call her the unloved queen. "I am poor, with barely enough food for myself," the unloved queen said. "But I'll share with the old woman."

The old woman was therefore taken to the unloved queen's home. The bed was already prepared for her and, oh, the old woman had barely rested in her wanderings, so she immediately fell asleep.

In the morning, the unloved queen gave the old woman two ears of corn. "This is your breakfast. Now I will go work in the field all day."

"Where are your pots?" asked the old woman. "I'll prepare a meal."

"Don't be silly. You're old and you have trouble walking. Just sit."

"I'm excellent at preparing dinner pots. Where can I find fuel?"

"No, no," said the unloved queen. "You can't fetch fuel. The forest is down that path over there. You shouldn't walk so far."

The old woman nodded. "Where is the field where you will be working?"

"Old woman, you can't walk to the field. The path is bumpy. See the tracks made by the cattle? They walk from the village to the field every morning and back every night." The unloved queen then left.

The old woman sat all alone in the unloved queen's home. That's when her four daughters, four sons, and their two dogs came out of her knee. They set to work at once. Two daughters pounded corn into meal. Two daughters fetched wood and water. All four sons and their two dogs went hunting and came back with an antelope—a duiker—that the whole family cleaned and prepared. They made a hearty meal of stewed meat and corn porridge. Then the daughters and sons and dogs went back inside the old woman's knee.

The old woman put the pot of food into a basket and followed the cattle tracks to the field.

"What are you doing?" said the unloved queen. "It must have been painful for you to walk here."

"I brought you food."

The unloved queen opened the basket and gasped. "How did you make this? All I left you with was two ears of corn." When the old woman merely smiled, the unloved queen sat down and enjoyed the food. The old woman watched her, still smiling. At the end of the day, they walked home together.

The next day was the same. And the day after that. And on and on. The unloved queen grew strong from the wonderful food and soon stopped mentioning how painful it must have been for the old woman to do all this work. She just thanked her, and the old woman smiled.

One day, the unloved queen went to the chief. "Please come to my home. I must show you something."

"I have better things to do," said the chief. He really didn't love this last queen at all.

"It's about the old woman."

"Don't complain. You took her in of your own free will."

"I'm not complaining. Quite the contrary." And she told him about the old woman's meals.

"What a story," said the chief. "This I have to see for myself."

The next day, the chief hid outside the unloved queen's home at midday. When the old woman went to the field carrying the basket, he followed. The old woman handed the basket to the unloved queen.

The chief ran up. "What's in the basket?"

"You know very well," said the unloved queen. "But since I have not cleaned my hands properly, I cannot uncover it to offer to you."

"I don't care about dirty hands!" The chief sniffed the air. "It smells tasty. Uncover it and I'll eat it all up."

FROM MEXICO TO AFRICA
Corn is indigenous to the Americas. It originated as a wild grain with small kernels, irregularly spaced on the cob, and may have first been cultivated in Mexico some 10,000 years ago. When Europeans traveled to the Americas in the years around 1500, one of the crops they brought back with them was corn. Corn was then introduced to Africa. Harvested corn can stay edible for long periods, so it became the food of choice for ships transporting enslaved African people to sugar plantations in the Caribbean islands and the Americas. Corn also became an important crop for many areas of Africa.

The unloved queen uncovered the basket and the chief ate the meal.

That night the chief thought and thought. This old woman clearly had a secret, and the chief was determined to figure it out. The next day, the chief returned to his hiding spot outside the unloved queen's home. But this time he came at dawn, to witness every step in the preparation of the meal.

What was that? Four young women came out of the unloved queen's home. They scurried off, as though they had work to do. Now four young men came out, with two dogs. They raced away. Soon enough the women and men and dogs returned with the makings for a fine meal. They all went inside the house.

The chief banged his fists on the door of the unloved queen's home.

Instantly, the old woman pointed at her knee. Her daughters and sons and their dogs disappeared inside that knee.

The chief entered without being bidden. "Where are those young women and young men?" He walked around the room.

"Who? I don't see anyone."

"They made that pot of food there. I saw them with my own eyes. And the women—oh, they were beautiful. Where have they gone?" But the old woman just looked at the chief as though he was speaking nonsense. Shaking his head, the chief went home and told one of his advisers what had happened.

"I'll catch them," said the adviser. And the next morning, he waited

in that hiding spot until the old woman's children came out the door. The adviser rushed at them.

The children immediately raced back into the house. By the time the adviser reached the door, they had already disappeared into the old woman's knee.

The adviser went back to the chief. "You're right, there are four young women and four young men. But I couldn't catch them."

"The young women were beauties," said the chief. "I will marry them. Figure out a way to catch them."

"Get a large cloth and some strong men," said the adviser. "Tomorrow, we'll catch them."

The next day, the chief and his adviser went with the large cloth and the strong men to hide outside the home of the unloved queen and the old woman. When the old woman's children came out the door, the adviser ran inside the house and covered the old woman with the large cloth and the strong men held the old woman captive inside that cloth. The old woman's children raced inside behind these intruders, but they couldn't reach their mother's knee; they couldn't disappear.

"Let me go!" called the old woman from inside the cloth.

"I won't harm you," said the chief. "Don't worry. I want to marry those young women."

"No," said the old woman. "They aren't yours for the taking."

"Of course they are," said the chief. "I am chief. They are beautiful. It's my right. But you must consent."

"I'll ask them what they want," said the old woman. "But first, what do you plan to do to me and my sons?"

"You can live here, with my little queen. Your sons can marry my daughters."

"If they choose to," said the old woman.

"Of course they'll choose to," said the chief. "My daughters are princesses."

"What about my sons' dogs?" asked the old woman.

"They can go wherever your sons want."

The old woman called out to her children. They all called back happily. So the old woman agreed.

The chief sent messengers to fetch all the people and all their cattle and bring them back to the village for a celebration. As soon as the people were all together, rains fell. Hard and fast. For the rest of the day, the old woman's children danced in that rain, slopping about in the mud and flapping their arms like spur-winged geese in spring.

"Now they are strong," said the old woman. "Dancing in the rain fortified them. Without that, they would have died."

The chief married the old woman's daughters, and his daughters married the old woman's sons.

The dogs stayed with the old woman and the unloved wife. Now that her knee was empty, the old woman walked with comfort. So the two women worked together in the fields, happy. Every once in a while, the dogs brought home a rabbit or a quail and they made a fancy meal. But on most days, they were content with corn porridge.

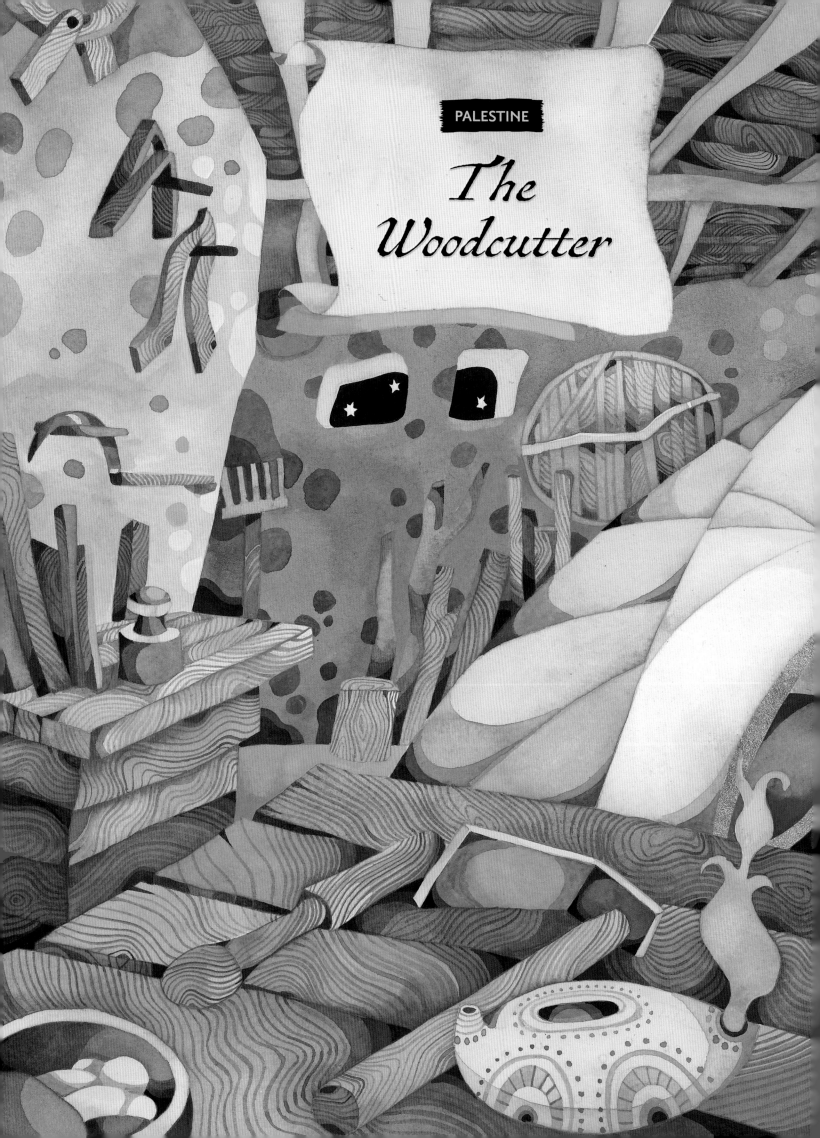

PALESTINE

The Woodcutter

woodcutter made his daily living by selling small bundles of wood. His was a meager existence; the money he earned each day paid for his food and nothing more. One morning, he roasted a handful of fava beans to munch on as he walked to the market to sell his wood.

Along the way, he passed the home of a rich man, who had a well outside. The poor woodcutter flipped a bean up into the air to catch in his mouth. But, oh no! The bean landed not on his tongue, but in the rich man's well.

> *Alas, my bean, my fava bean,*
> *Without you I grow far too lean.*

The woodcutter chanted those words repeatedly, and he cried.

"Hush, old man," came a voice from inside the well.

"Your noise hurts our ears," came another voice.

"What on earth's the matter with you?" came a third voice.

"I won't hush," called the woodcutter to the denizens of the well. "Give me back my fava bean." And he chanted even louder:

> *Alas, my bean, my fava bean,*
> *Without you I grow far too lean.*

"What a lot of nonsense over a plain old fava bean!"

"Here, take this wooden bowl. Whatever you tell it to fill with, it will fill."

A wooden bowl came flying up out of the well and landed in the woodcutter's hands.

"And don't just ask for fava beans, you simpleton."

The woodcutter turned right around and went home. He locked the door behind him and set the bowl on the table. Would it work? "Fill with rice." He took a deep breath. "And meat on top." He took a deeper breath. "And yogurt on the very top!"

The wooden bowl filled to the brim. The woodcutter ate so much, he fell off his bench and slept right there on the floor. When he finally woke, he told the bowl, "Fill with cracked wheat, and noodles and tomato sauce," which it promptly did. After that, the woodcutter didn't cut wood anymore. Instead, when he was hungry, he told the bowl to fill. Then he ate as much as he liked and threw the rest away.

After many days of this routine, the woodcutter became bored. He hadn't been to the market in a long time. He needed some fun. But he wouldn't risk taking the bowl with him, for fear of losing it. And he wouldn't risk leaving the bowl home, for fear of someone taking it. So he went to his neighbor's house and said, "Dear neighbor, please would you take care of my wooden bowl while I go into town?"

"What? Just leave that old bowl at home."

"No, no, it must be guarded. And you must promise not to ruin it."

"And exactly how would I ruin an old bowl?"

"Why, by asking it to fill with rice and meat. Don't do that. Just let it be. I'll come home in a couple of days to fetch it."

As soon as the woodcutter was out of sight, the neighbor, who had a brain a bit cleverer than that of the woodcutter, said to the bowl, "Fill up with rice and meat." The bowl did, of course. "Add some yogurt on top." And the bowl did. The neighbor's family ate and ate, until they could barely move.

A couple of days later, the woodcutter appeared at the neighbor's door. "I've come for my bowl."

"Here it is," said the neighbor, handing the woodcutter a wooden bowl. But that wasn't the magic bowl at all; it was an ordinary bowl from the neighbor's shelf.

The woodcutter was none the wiser. He went home, locked the door, and set the bowl on the table. "Fill with rice and meat and yogurt," he said. But the bowl did not fill. "Fill with noodles and tomato sauce," he said. Still the bowl did not fill. "Fill with lentils. Fill with fava beans. Fill with anything, please. I'm hungry." The bowl sat there empty.

The woodcutter carried the bowl back to the neighbor. "What did you do to my bowl?"

"Nothing," said the neighbor. "What's the problem?"

"Bah!" said the woodcutter. He carried the bowl back to the well that had given him the bowl in the first place, and threw it down inside. Then he chanted as he cried:

Alas, my bean, my fava bean,

Without you I grow far too lean.

"What? Is that you again, foolish woodcutter?"

"What's the matter with you?"

"We gave you the wooden bowl! You should be happy."

"I was happy," the woodcutter said. "But the bowl got ruined. It doesn't work anymore."

"All right, all right. Take this mill, instead."

"Turn the handle to the right, and it will grind gold."

"Turn the handle to the left, and it will grind silver."

The woodcutter took the mill home, locked the door, set it on the table, and turned the handle. Gold and silver! Amazing! This was far better than the wooden bowl. Every few days, he filled his pockets and went off to the city to have fun until he ran out of money.

But after a month of fun time, the woodcutter fell into a funk.

Anyone could come along and steal the mill while he was in the city. Then where would he be? The safe thing to do was leave it at a neighbor's house. But not the neighbor he'd left the bowl with—no way, not him.

The woodcutter knocked on another neighbor's door. "Dear neighbor, please would you take care of my mill while I go to town for a few days?"

"What? It's a mill. What kind of care does it need?"

"It must be guarded. And you must promise not to use it."

"I have a mill of my own. Why would I use yours?"

"Why, to get gold by turning the handle to the right, or silver by turning the handle to the left. Don't do that. Just let it be. I'll come home in a couple of days to fetch it."

As soon as the woodcutter was out of sight, what do you think this neighbor did? You're right: She turned the handle of the wood-cutter's mill, first to the right, then to the left. Gold and silver! The neighbor's family went to town for the rest of the day to have some fun of their own.

A couple of days later, the woodcutter appeared at the neighbor's door. "I've come for my mill."

"Here it is," said the neighbor, handing the woodcutter a mill. Do you think it was the woodcutter's mill? Right again: This was the family's old mill.

The woodcutter went home, locked the door, and set the mill on the table. He turned the handle to the right. To the left. To the right. To the left. He kept that up for hours, until his arms ached horribly.

"Bah!" said the woodcutter. "Bah and double bah!" He carried the mill back to the well and threw it down inside. Then he chanted as he cried:

> Alas, my bean, my fava bean,
> Without you I grow far too lean.

"What? Are you totally berserk?"

"We gave you the wooden bowl. We gave you the little mill."

"What else could you want?"

"They're gone," the woodcutter said. "I think people robbed me."

"Really? So you finally figured that out."

"Here's the solution: Take this stick."

"Tell the stick to beat the robbers until they return your things."

The woodcutter took the stick to the home of the neighbor he had left his wooden bowl with. "Give me back my bowl," he said.

"What? We already gave it to you."

"You're asking for trouble," said the woodcutter, and he chanted:

> It's time, my stick, my magic stick,
> To find the truth through smash and kick.

Well, that stick went right to work, knocking the neighbor around.

"Stop!" called the neighbor, piteously. "I have your wretched wooden bowl. It's there, on the shelf. Take it away."

The woodcutter took the bowl home and tried it out. Yes, this was definitely his magic bowl. Then he went to the second neighbor's house. "Give me back my mill," he said.

"Mill? We already returned it to you."

Again, the woodcutter chanted:

> It's time, my stick, my magic stick,
> To find the truth through smash and kick.

Again, that stick did its job, and the woodcutter went home with his mill. He lived out the rest of his life with plenty to eat and plenty to spend on fun. That's a lovely benefit of magic, you see.

A PRECIOUS RESOURCE
The region in southwestern Asia where this story takes place is dry a good part of the year, which means that wells are prized as a source of the most essential good: water. The well in this story has supernatural spirits living in it that produce magical objects, but those objects are not uniformly "good." The bowl produces food, so it is positive. The mill produces gold and silver, which can be used for positive or negative purposes. The stick beats people into submission until they tell the truth, another mixed purpose. Perhaps the spirits in this well are Arab *jinn* (genies). These are intermediary beings—neither gods nor humans—that can shift toward or away from good.

KURDISH, WESTERN ASIA

The Girl With Seven Brothers

even girls sat in a circle making lace when one of them passed gas loudly.

"It wasn't me," said one girl. "I swear on my brother's life."

"Not me," said another girl. "I swear on my two brothers' lives."

"Nor me," said a third. "I swear on my three brothers' lives."

They went the full circle, each swearing on one more brother's life. The seventh girl said, "Not me. I swear on my mother's hair." Everyone laughed and guessed she was the guilty one—which she was.

The girl went home and told her mother, "Our family is too small—just you and me."

"Wrong! You have seven brothers, who live far away."

"Really? I must go visit them. How do I get there?"

"I'll make you a donkey. No matter what you see along the way, stay on the donkey."

The mother, who knew fine magic, swooped up dust and fashioned a donkey.

The girl was well down the road when she saw something shiny on the ground. Gold! She slid off that donkey to grab it. As her feet hit the ground, the donkey turned to dust and the gold disappeared!

The girl returned home and confessed. Her mother made her a second donkey and gave the same warning. The girl set out again, trying not to look down, but, oh my, what was that in the road? Money! She slid off the donkey and—poof!—the animal turned to dust and the money vanished.

Again, the girl confessed. Again, her mother made a donkey from dust. "This is the last donkey. Don't get off it!"

The girl had never been good at following directions. So this time she kept her eyes shut for days, until the donkey stopped. When she opened her eyes, a big house stood before her. She went inside. No one was home but a cat. The girl cleaned the house, made dinner, and set out seven plates on the table. The cat meowed the whole time, but the girl was too busy to pet him. Finished, she hid behind a pillar.

The seven brothers came home.

"What? The house is clean."

"Dinner is made."

"And it's delicious."

"You, brother with the seven eyes, keep watch while we sleep. Find out who did this."

While six brothers slept, the girl came out from behind the pillar and set about cleaning up the mess from dinner. The seven-eyed brother woke the others and they caught her. "Don't be alarmed," she said. "I'm your sister."

"Fantastic!"

"Thank you for cooking such a wonderful dinner."

"And for cleaning."

"There's always room for family," said the youngest brother. "Why not live with us?"

"But be careful: There's a horrid giantess."

"Don't go near her castle."

"She eats people."

Every day the brothers went into the forest to chop wood. Every day the sister cleaned house and cooked. Things were going well for everyone except the cat. He needed petting. To spite the girl, he sprayed the fire until it went out.

Soon the girl shivered. The fire had gone out! She walked and walked in search of new coals and came upon the castle of the giantess. Her brothers had warned her, so she hid and watched. Before long, the giantess came outside and disappeared into the woods. She heard sweet voices from within, so the girl knocked on the door.

SIGNIFICANT SEVEN
The number seven is like a drumbeat in this story. Its appearance might suggest this is a story indigenous to the Kurds, since seven is a venerated number in the ancient Kurdish religion called the Cult of Angels. The most well-known branch of this religion to have survived into modern times is Yezidism. Both the ancient and the present religions include a belief in seven angels who protect the universe from seven evil forces. Zoroastrianism is another religion that has thrived among Kurdish people for many centuries. The number seven is important to it as well. In Zoroastrianism, there is one creator, known as Ahura Mazda, who created six beneficent immortals, or archangels, to help govern everything—a total of seven divine beings.

The door opened
and seven girls stared at
her. "Who are you?"

"I need coals."

"Mother counts the
coals. She'll know if any
go missing."

"Please," said the girl.
"I'm chilled to the bone
at home."

The daughters of the
giantess gave her coals.
"Run now, so Mother
won't see you."

The girl turned to
run. But she tripped,
and a thread from her
sash got tangled in a bush, so that the sash unraveled as she ran.

When the giantess came home, she shouted, "Where is the human
I smell?"

"A girl was here," said the daughters. "But she lives far away."

The giantess stomped outside and found the thread caught in the
branches. She followed it to the house of the seven brothers. "Open up!"

"No. You'll eat me," said the girl.

"Well, stick out your finger for me to suck blood from. Otherwise
I'll die of hunger."

"I don't think that's the best idea."

"How about another idea?" the giantess said. "I'll kill whoever
comes to this house."

The girl truly loved her brothers. She stuck her finger out through
the keyhole. The giantess drank her blood until the girl fainted away.

Every day the brothers went to work. Every day the giantess came and sucked blood from their sister's finger until the girl fainted. One day the brothers came home early and found their sister unconscious. What terrible secret did she have?

The next day, instead of going to work, they hid outside and watched the house. The giantess arrived and their sister stuck her finger through the keyhole for the giantess to suck. The brothers rushed the giantess and killed her. Then their sister told the whole story.

When they heard about the daughters of the giantess, they smiled. Those girls had given their sister coals, so they must be kind. Further, there were seven of them—one for each brother. The brothers went to the castle and married the daughters of the giantess.

They all lived in the castle now, and the sister figured she'd have seven new sisters. Instead, her brothers' wives made her do all the chores alone and hardly talked to her. The girl was wretched.

One day the daughters of the giantess gave the girl a drink of water. But that water was tainted. They had taken a hair from their dead mother's body and placed it in the water. When the girl drank it, that hair grew. And multiplied. Day after day, more hairs grew inside the girl's belly, until she became lumpy and could hardly walk.

"Look," said one of the daughters of the giantess to her husband. "Your sister is sick."

"She can't clean," said another to her husband.

"She can't cook," said a third to her husband.

"She's useless," said a fourth very softly.

"She doesn't have long to live anyway," whispered a fifth.

"Kill her now," breathed a sixth.

The brothers were spellbound by their wives' words. They decided that the dreadful task should fall to the youngest brother.

The youngest brother said to his sister, "I have to cut wood. Come with me."

When they were deep in the forest, the youngest brother said, "Let's stop for a rest." The girl lay down and fell asleep. The youngest brother watched her gentle face. How could he possibly kill her? Still, he mustn't let her return to the castle, because his wife would get angry—and she was scary when she got angry. So he tied acorns together with a string and hung them from a tree. When the wind blew, they clacked together and sounded like someone chopping wood far away. This way when his sister woke, she'd listen and wait for him to return. That would give him enough time to get away. She'd never be able to find her way back to the castle on her own.

When the girl woke, she saw the cluster of acorns and figured out what her brother had done. How mean! Well, her mother had taught her a little magic; she put a curse on her brother:

May you step on a snake spine that pierces your shoe.
And hobble in pain, till your only sister heals you.

She wobbled through the forest and came upon a village.

A man invited her inside to rest. "Poor girl. What ails you?"

"I don't know. Maybe ... oh dear ... maybe I've been poisoned."

"Here, take a whiff of this." He opened a clay jar. "These are vegetables pickled for seven years. Vermin hate their smell."

The girl breathed deep and held her breath. Soon snake after snake after snake slithered out of her mouth, and she was healed.

The villager fell in love with the girl and she with him. They married and were happy.

One day a visitor came limping into the village. The girl said, "Sir, why do you limp?"

"I stepped on a snake spine years ago. No one can heal me."

"Let me try."

The girl pierced the bottom of the man's foot with a needle and dug out the snake spine. And his foot healed.

"You're my youngest brother," she said.

Each explained to the other all that had happened since that day in the woods. It turned out the brothers were miserable because of the giantess's hideous daughters.

So the girl and her husband and her youngest brother went to the giantess's castle, gathered the other six brothers, and all of them went back to the girl's original home. Lo and behold, their mother still lived there. They moved back in and shared all the chores. That's where they are today, all together, one big family.

TURKEY

Three Magic Gifts

wo brothers were left on their own after their parents died. They split the inheritance half and half. Older Brother invested his money in a shop and worked hard. Younger Brother spent his money on games and candy until nothing remained.

"Hey, Older Brother, help me out," said Younger Brother.

Older Brother gave Younger Brother money. And neither changed their habits.

Within months, Younger Brother was destitute again. "Hey, Older Brother, help me out."

Older Brother did. This routine continued for a while, until Older Brother realized that soon he'd have nothing, just like Younger Brother. His only hope was to run away to Egypt, where he could start over without the burden of Younger Brother. He sold his shop, bought a ticket on a ship, and hid away belowdecks until sailing.

Younger Brother somehow heard what Older Brother was up to. He snuck onto the ship and hid away belowdecks until sailing, too.

When the ship set sail, both brothers went up on deck. *Oh no,* thought Older Brother, *I cannot stand this. Younger Brother will ruin me.*

As the ship landed in Egypt, Older Brother said, "I'll get mules to carry us inland. Wait here."

Younger Brother sat down to wait. But Older Brother never returned, of course. Younger Brother finally set out after him. He walked with small steps for half a year and looked back. Well, he hadn't come very far at all. He walked with big steps for another half a year and wound up at the foot of a mountain, where three men were arguing.

"What's the matter?" asked Younger Brother.

"Our father died and left behind a turban, a whip, and a prayer rug," said one of the men.

"They're magic," said the second man. "Whoever puts on the

turban goes invisible, as does everything he touches. Whoever sits on the carpet and cracks the whip flies off like a bird."

"All three magic gifts should stay together with only one of us," said the third man. "Me." And the men started arguing again.

"I'll solve this," said Younger Brother. "I'll shoot an arrow and you three can run after it. Whoever brings back the arrow gets all three gifts." He shot the arrow and the men raced off after it. But Younger Brother was a sneak; he quickly put on the turban, sat on the carpet, and cracked the whip. He flew away and wound up outside the gate of a big city in Egypt.

People in the city were excited; there was mystery in the air. The sultan's daughter disappeared every night and no one knew where she went. Whoever figured that out would get to marry the princess and own half the kingdom. Younger Brother immediately went to the palace and claimed he'd solve the mystery. He posted himself outside the princess's bedroom to keep watch all night. But he soon began snoring.

The princess peeked out of her room at the man outside her door. He certainly seemed to be asleep. To be sure, though, she jabbed the soles of his feet with a pin. Since he didn't stir, she picked up the candle beside him and snuck out the side door.

Younger Brother had been pretending to sleep, of course. He put on the turban, grabbed the magic whip, and tucked the magic carpet under his arm. Invisible, he ran as fast as he could until he saw the princess up ahead sitting in a bowl on top of the head of an enormous man. Why it was a magic man—a Dew! Younger Brother leaped up into the bowl.

"Why are you jumping around up there?" asked the Dew.

"I haven't moved at all," said the princess. "It's you who shakes the bowl."

The Dew took a few steps. "You are more than twice as heavy tonight than you usually are," said the Dew. "You're crushing me."

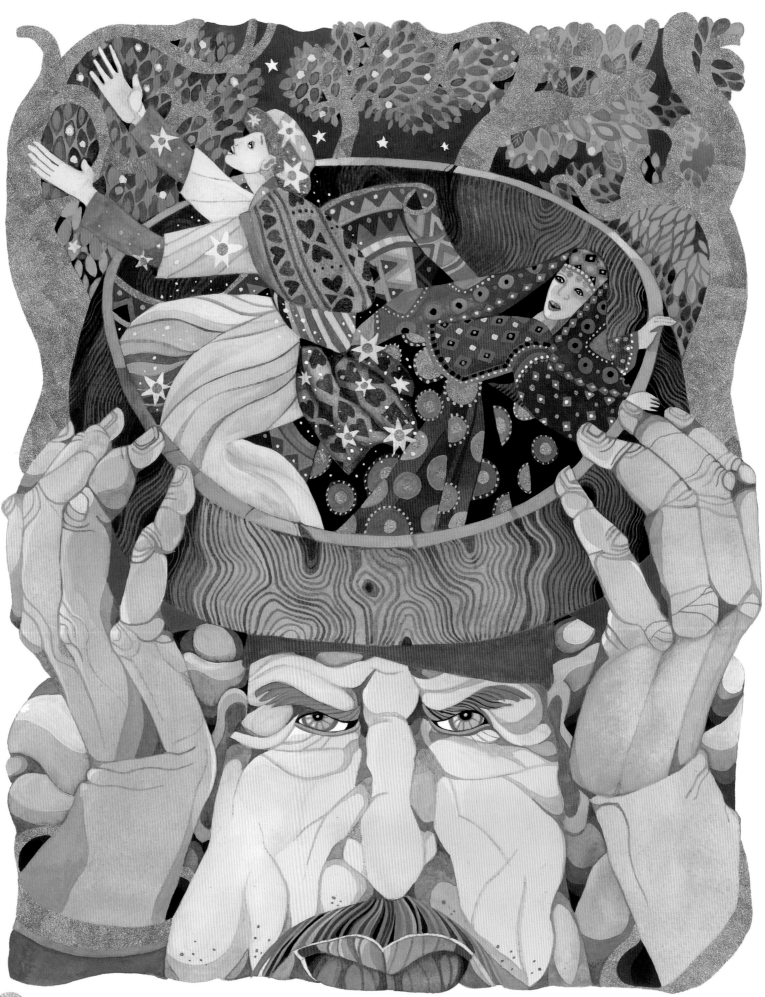

"Don't be silly," said the princess. "I'm how I've always been."

The Dew walked out into a garden. Younger Brother's eyes grew round with greed; the trees in this garden were silver and studded with diamonds. He broke off a branch.

"Alas!" screamed the tree. "A human has hurt me. Alas!"

"I didn't hurt the tree," said the princess.

The Dew was puzzled, but not enough to make him hesitate. He walked on to a second garden.

Younger Brother's eyes nearly popped out of his head; the trees here were gold and studded with precious stones. He broke off a branch.

"Wretched world!" screamed the tree. "A human has hurt me. Wretched world!"

"Not me," said the princess.

Again, the Dew was puzzled, but he had a job to do, so he walked on over a bridge and arrived at a palace.

The princess climbed down from the bowl and went to the crowd of servants awaiting her. They gave her a pair of jeweled slippers. The princess put one on, but Younger Brother, who had followed her down from the bowl, grabbed the other, which immediately went invisible. The princess searched for it, then stamped her foot in anger—which was unfortunate, since that was the foot without a shoe—and she hurt herself. Angrier than ever, she ran into the palace all the way to the room of the Dew King, who kissed heaven and earth every morning.

"Why so late, Princess?" asked the Dew King.

"A human was guarding my bedroom," said the princess. "An irritating man. Everything is irritating today."

"Relax. All is well now." The Dew King placed his hand on his heart and smiled a welcome to the princess. "Let's eat delicious, freezing sherbet." He pointed to a servant, who immediately brought two diamond-studded cups of sherbet.

As the princess reached for her cup, Younger Brother knocked

AN ANCIENT TREAT
Sherbet is a frozen dessert that originated as an icy drink among the wealthy in ancient Persia. In a land that is hot much of the year, this cold mix of fruit and sugar, and often milk or cream, was a welcome luxury. At its largest, the Persian Empire stretched from northern Africa to northwestern India and included many areas that are now part of Turkey. So while you might have been surprised at the Dew King's offering of sherbet, it was, indeed, an offering befitting a princess.

it from the servant's hand. It fell and broke. Younger Brother quickly pocketed a shard from the cup.

"See!" cried the princess. "Everything is wrong today!"

"Hush, little one," said the Dew King. "Let's have a fine meal."

So the servants set out a banquet. Younger Brother was delighted. He grabbed meat from one platter, rice from another. The food was disappearing quickly.

"Someone's here with us," said the Dew King, anxiously. "Give me a kiss and hurry home."

As the princess moved toward the Dew King, Younger Brother stepped between them and pushed them apart.

"Hurry, Servant, take the princess home," called the Dew King.

The princess climbed up and sat in the bowl on the Dew servant's head again. Younger Brother grabbed a sword hanging from the wall and slew the Dew King. Then he sat on his magic carpet, cracked his magic whip, and flew back to the princess's palace.

By the time the princess got home, Younger Brother was outside her bedroom, snoring. The princess jabbed his feet with the pin again, this time just for spite.

In the morning, the sultan asked Younger Brother if he had solved the mystery. "I have," said Younger Brother. "Call all the residents of the city together to hear the answer."

Once all the people were gathered in the market square, Younger Brother told what had happened the night before.

"He's lying," said the princess.

Younger Brother then produced the silver branch studded with diamonds, the gold branch studded with precious stones, the princess's jeweled slipper, and the shard from the fancy sherbet cup. Before the sultan could speak, Younger Brother spied Older Brother in the crowd. He ran after him. Older Brother took off in fear. But Younger Brother tackled him and dragged him back to the sultan.

"Give the princess to my brother in marriage," said Younger Brother. "Give him half your kingdom." For, you see, Younger Brother really did love Older Brother and wanted to be near him the rest of his life. And he had no need of a wife or half a kingdom. With the magic turban, the magic carpet, and the magic whip, Younger Brother could manage to get whatever he needed in life.

"Me, marry the princess?" said Older Brother. He stepped toward her. "Oh, you seem an interesting sort. Do you want to marry me?"

The princess had been under a spell cast by the Dew King. Now that he was dead, she remembered him with disgust. And this funny man standing in front of her, who was asking to marry her, well, he seemed all right. A lot better than the Dew King. So she smiled. The wedding celebration lasted 40 days and 40 nights.

Yes, this was a fine ending to things, thought the princess and Younger Brother and even Older Brother.

JEWISH DIASPORA

The Gobbler

n the castle lived the king, the queen, and the prince. All very ordinary, or as ordinary as castles go. They had delicious food and splendid clothes and tutors for everything, from geography to poetry, from biology to astronomy. Yes, an ordinary royal family.

Until one morning the prince walked into the grand hall, circled his parents' thrones, looked sideways at them, and gobbled.

"What?" said the queen.

"I'm a turkey," said the prince.

"You're a prince," said the king.

"A turkey prince," said the prince. "Gobble gobble."

The queen laughed. "What a bizarre joke."

"Gobble gobble."

The king wrinkled his nose. "What young people won't do these days to get a little attention."

The prince walked out of the room, jerking his head this way and that. "Gobble."

That night at dinner the prince arrived naked.

"You don't have any clothes on," said the queen.

"Turkeys don't wear clothes."

"Oh, I guess they don't."

The prince came up to the table and examined the food. When he got to the bread, he was so excited, he pecked like crazy and smashed his nose. "Gobble. Gobble, gobble, gobble."

"Your poor nose," said the king. "Being a turkey is hazardous. Plus, going around with no clothes on means people might feel embarrassed to visit you."

"It's far worse than that, dear son," said the queen. "We miss talking with you. We don't understand gobble. And if you eat only bread, how will you stay healthy?"

The turkey prince pecked at bread crumbs on the floor. "Gobble."

In the weeks that followed, the king sent out his courtiers to find doctors and philosophers and sages, anyone who might be able to help the prince figure out how to stay healthy. The king was ready to pay a high price.

Doctors and philosophers and sages came and went, to no avail.

Meanwhile the turkey prince developed a new routine. Every morning the cook scattered crumbs on the floor under the table for him to peck at. When he was satisfied, he went outside and dusted himself thoroughly with dirt, then flapped his arms furiously for an hour, and finally hopped up into a tree to roost for the rest of the day.

The queen moaned her grief. The king sighed his sorrow. The turkey prince gobbled.

One day a wise man showed up in the royal garden and gazed at the turkey prince high in a tree. "I'll help," he said at last. "No charge. But on the condition that I am allowed to do whatever I want—no one can interfere."

The king and queen nodded hopefully.

The next morning at breakfast, the turkey prince found a naked man poking around the floor under the table. It was the wise man.

"What are you doing here?" asked the turkey prince.

"What are you doing here?" answered the man.

"Eating. I'm a turkey."

"So am I." The man pecked at the crumbs.

"Gobble?" said the turkey prince.

"Gobble!" said the wise man.

The king looked at the queen. "Another one!" he whispered. The queen blinked.

On the third day the wise man called the king over. "Could I have a shirt, please?"

The king raised his eyebrows in surprise.

"Turkeys can wear shirts," said the wise man. He turned to the turkey prince. "Don't you agree?"

The turkey prince did agree.

So both of them put on shirts.

On the sixth day the wise man called the king over. "Could I have pants, please?" He looked over at the turkey prince. "Who's to say turkeys can't wear pants, right?"

The turkey prince barely hesitated.

So both of them put on pants.

On the ninth day the wise man asked for human food. And a chair at the table. And some good conversation. "Where's it written that turkeys can't enjoy decent food, and comfortable chairs, and delightful conversation?" he said to the turkey prince.

The turkey prince agreed.

Soon the turkey prince behaved like a human being all day long. He knew he was still a turkey—we know these truths about ourselves. But he ate human food and wore human clothes and talked with humans. He found those things did hold a certain charm and comfort for him, after all.

Still, every so often, he made a little gobble.

BIRD RULES
This story belongs not to a particular land but to Jewish people, wherever they are. It revolves around what a turkey can do. Some birds are deemed "kosher," meaning that according to Jewish law they are "clean" and, so, fit for human consumption. The Hebrew Bible gives a list of forbidden (non-kosher) birds. But if a new bird comes along, sometimes there is confusion over whether it is kosher. That happened when the North American turkey was introduced in the 1500s into Europe. Eventually, farm-raised turkeys were accepted as kosher, although there is still controversy over whether wild ones are.

RUSSIA

The Gold
Fish

An old man and his old wife lived in a small hut on an island in the ocean. They had close to nothing: a bed, a table, benches, and a net. Every day, the old man threw that net into the ocean and dragged it back with fish. It was a life of raw poverty. But they didn't starve, and they had a roof over their heads.

One day the man threw his net into the water, and when he went to pull it out, he found it exceedingly heavy. Excited, he dragged as hard as he could. What? The net held only a single fish, the color of gold.

The fish cried out, "Please don't eat me. Set me free, and I'll grant whatever you wish."

Poor little fish!

"I don't want anything of you, Fishie. Go back to your waters." And the man threw the fish back into the ocean.

When he got home, he told his wife what had happened.

"You fool! You had a chance—a grand chance—and you didn't take it." The old woman berated the old man all night long. "You could have at least asked for bread! I'd love to eat bread—a whole loaf of bread."

She badgered the old man until he couldn't stand it anymore. He went to the ocean and called, "Fishie, Fishie, beautiful gold Fishie, stand up out of the water."

"Is that you, old man?" The fish swam along the shore. "What do you want?"

"My wife wants bread."

The fish laughed. "Go home. There's plenty of bread."

By the time the old man got home, his wife was gnawing greedily on a giant loaf of bread. But before the old man could take a bite, his wife said, "We need a trough. Ours broke. How can I do my washing without a trough?"

The old man shrugged. It was a tough question.

"Go back to the fish! Ask for a trough. Go! Go, go, go!"

So the old man went to the ocean and called, "Fishie, Fishie, beautiful gold Fishie, stand up out of the water."

"Ha! You again." The fish swam close. "What do you want?"

"My wife needs a new trough."

The fish said, "Pah! Go home. There's a trough awaiting you."

By the time the old man got home, his wife was eyeing a new trough … critically. "What good is a trough if our house falls down?"

"Huh?" The man looked up at the ceiling. Was their house falling down? He hadn't noticed.

"Always the fool, that's you. Go to the fish. Right now! Get us a new house. A strong one."

The old man returned to the ocean. "Fishie …"

At the very first call, that gold fish swam up. "What's it this time, old man?"

"My wife says our hut is falling down. She wants a new one."

"Go home," said the fish. "See what's there."

The old man returned and … amazing! Where his little hut had stood, there now stood a sturdy house of oak with intricate carvings all around the windows and all along the overhanging eaves and all down the sides and front of the fine door.

"Fool, fool, super fool," screamed his wife, stomping around the big hall. "Being a peasant is ridiculous. I want to be governor. Go tell the fish! Tell him everyone should bow to me."

"Fishie!" called the old man. "Fishie!"

"You again. What does she want?"

THE CRAFT OF CARVING
Russia has a long tradition of folk art, including woodcarving, which pops up in this story just briefly. Wooden homes in both cities and the countryside were once decorated with carved geometrical shapes or interlocking vines or cameo-like figures. Tables and cradles and chests, bowls and ladles and jugs—all the ordinary things of peasant life became extraordinary as people sat around the hearth in the long winters of the Russian forests, carving, carving, carving.

"She wants to be governor, so everyone will bow to her."

"Does she now?" The fish didn't purse his lips, because he didn't have the kind of lips that purse. But if you recognized fish expressions, you'd know this fish was less than pleased. "Go on home, old man. Go to your wife, the governor."

The man went home, but oh! The lovely carved oak house had been replaced by a huge stone house. Servants shoed horses in the court-yard. Cooks prepared beets and potatoes, served with aromatic black breads. And his wife sat in a high-backed chair dressed in a gown of red-and-gold flowered brocade.

"Dear wife …"

"Get that miserable fool out of my sight!" said the wife to her servants.

The servants dragged the old man to the stable and whipped him. From then on, the stable was his home. By day, he joined the servants in keeping the yards clean.

After a while, the old woman governor summoned the old man. "Governing is a bore. I want to be Queen, with nothing to do but stand on a balcony and listen to the band play and know everyone's hurrahs are for me. Yes! That would suit me just fine."

The old man stared at her.

"What are you waiting for? Tell that fish!"

"Fishie!" called the old man from the shore.

If the fish had not been such a polite sort, he might have answered, "Don't you 'fishie' me." But he was polite. "Speak," he said.

"She wants to be queen."

"Go home."

And, of course, the old woman now lived in a majestic castle with a roof as gold as the fish. How she passed her day, the old man hardly knew, for the servants who lived in the stable hardly ever set eyes on the queen.

One day the old woman queen summoned the old man again. "The ocean is bigger than the land, more important than the land. I should rule the ocean. All the waters, all the fishes, they should obey me. Go along now. Go tell your fish."

"Fishie!" called the old man.

The fish did not come.

"Fishie!" called the old man. "Fishie, my friend."

The fish did not come.

"Fishie, Fishie, Fishie!" called the old man. "Please, Fishie."

Waves came small, then large, then towering. The wind roared, the sea-foam whipped, the skies darkened. And the fish appeared. "Old man, old man, what do you want?"

"My wife wants to control the waves. She wants to command the fishes. She wants to be ruler of the whole ocean."

The fish dove. Without a word.

The old man went home.

What do you think he found?

His little old hut.

His little old wife in her raggedy old dress.

And no food on the table.

He picked up his net and went back to fishing.

He caught fish day after day. But never again one the color of gold.

CHUKCHI, RUSSIAN ARCTIC

The Girl and the Moon Spirit

ar north in the Arctic lands, a Chukchi man had an only daughter. She guarded the reindeer herd in all kinds of weather. Now and then she rode on her special reindeer back to camp to get food, but other than that she spent the long hours of day and night only with the herd.

One night her special reindeer said, "Look, girl of mine, look at the sky. See the Moon Spirit."

The girl saw the Moon Spirit gliding down in his sledge, pulled by two reindeer. "Why is he coming here?" asked the girl.

"To kidnap you," said the reindeer.

"No! I don't want to go up into the sky."

The reindeer pawed a hole in the snow. "Get in. Quick."

The girl jumped into the hole and squatted. The reindeer covered her with snow.

The Moon Spirit landed. "Where did that girl go? I know I saw her." He tramped all around, right past the hole where the girl was hiding. But it looked like nothing more than a snowdrift. He got back into his sledge. "All right, I give up for now. But I'll come back and get her." His sledge flew up into the sky and away.

The girl's reindeer now raked the snow off the hole, and the girl stepped out. "We must return to camp, before the Moon Spirit sees me again." She rode her reindeer as fast as they could go, leaving a swirl of snow behind. When they got to camp, the girl ran to her father's *yaranga,* that wonderful round tent of thick reindeer skin that she had grown up in. But her father wasn't home. This was awful! She needed help.

"Hide," called her reindeer. "Hide or the Moon Spirit will get you."

"But where?"

"I can turn you into a block of stone."

The girl shook her head. "He'll know it's me."

"I can turn you into a hammer."

"He'll know!"

"I can turn you into a tent pole for a yaranga."

"Can't you understand? He'll know it's me."

"How about something different. Something hot. I can turn you into an oil lamp."

"All right."

The girl squatted and closed her eyes. Her reindeer smacked the ground with his hoof. All at once, in her place was an oil lamp. It lit up the whole yaranga.

Just then, the Moon Spirit arrived in the camp. The disappearance of the girl was driving him to distraction. He knew he had seen her, clear as day. He had searched through the reindeer herd, to no avail. She must be hiding in this camp. He tramped all around the yaranga. Then he entered it. He searched among the pile of stones and the tools and the tent poles. The girl was nowhere. He didn't give the oil lamp a second thought because it sat there shining, just like the moon did—it felt ordinary.

The girl, who was now an oil lamp, shivered in fear and excitement because the Moon Spirit was so close.

"Where, oh where, did that girl go? This is extraordinary! All right, I give up again. But I'll come back to get that girl." The Moon Spirit went out the flap of the tent.

But the girl's excitement got the better of her. She couldn't stop a nervous laugh from bursting forth, and that turned her back into her true self. "Ha, ha! Here I am!"

The Moon Spirit rushed back into the yaranga. But the girl had turned into the oil lamp again. He raced around the yaranga, inspecting every object. The girl was nowhere. Still, he would not stop searching. He touched everything again, and again, and again. Days passed, and

LIGHT OF THE MOON

The sun and the moon are of enormous importance to people across the northern Arctic, including the Chukchi of what is now the Russian Arctic. In the dead of winter, the sun never rises above the horizon; this period is called the polar night. In the peak of summer, the sun never fully dips below the horizon; this period is called the polar day. But the moon comes and goes all year long, being visible day and night for about two weeks at a time, then invisible for about two weeks at a time. So the moon is a more constant source of light (reflected light from the sun) than the sun itself; thus, it's no surprise that the moon is the subject of many legends across different Arctic communities.

the Moon Spirit grew thin and weak. He stumbled now, barely able to walk.

The girl took heart: Why, this Moon Spirit wasn't scary; he was powerless! She transformed into her true form and rushed at him, pinning him on his back. She bound his hands and legs.

"Careful or you'll kill me," said the Moon Spirit. "But you know, maybe you should kill me. I was going to steal you away from your home, after all. So go ahead, kill me. But first, please wrap me in a blanket. I'm so cold, I'm about to freeze."

"You, freeze? I don't believe it. You wander endlessly. You have no yaranga. I don't believe you need a blanket."

"Let me go then. Let me live outside, homeless. Let me light up the night so it's bright as day. Let me measure out time in months—the Moon of the Old Stag, then the Moon of the Newborn Calves, then the Water Moon, the Leafy Moon, the Warm Moon, the Horn Shedding Moon, the Reindeer Love Moon, the Moon of the First Winter, and finally, the Moon of Shortening Days."

The girl did love the glow of the moon at night. She did love the way the moon measured out her life. "If I let you go, will you simply come after me once you feel strong again?"

"No. I'll leave you in peace, even though you are so brilliant you make me long for you. But I will never come down from the sky again. Let me go."

So the girl did. And the Moon Spirit went up into the sky and never came down again. See him there? Right there, shining so that the Chukchi and everyone else on Earth can fall asleep in his glow.

KOREA

*The Gentleman
and the Tiger*

 young gentleman was journeying by horseback when a may beetle flying by said, "May I come with you?"

"Why not?"

So the young gentleman, with the may beetle settled in the horse's mane, continued his journey when an egg rolling by said, "Maybe I come with you?

"Why not?"

So the young gentleman, with the may beetle and the egg settled in the horse's mane, continued his journey when a crab sidling by said, "May I come with you?"

"Why not?"

So the young gentleman, with the may beetle, the egg, and the crab settled in the horse's mane, continued his journey when a rice ladle hopping by said, "May I come with you?"

"Why not?"

So the young gentleman, with the may beetle, the egg, the crab, and the rice ladle settled in the horse's mane, continued his journey when an awl zigzagging by said, "May I come with you?"

"Why not?"

The horse's mane was getting rather cozy by now. But the young gentleman was a friendly sort. So when a mortar came tumbling by and asked to come along, he welcomed it, just as he welcomed a straw mat flapping by and then a wooden pack-carrier stalking by.

When evening came, the young gentleman with the may beetle, the egg, the crab, the rice ladle, the awl, the mortar, the straw mat, and the pack-carrier arrived at the foot of a mountain where a house stood. The gentleman knocked at the entrance. When no one answered, he went in, timidly. "Hello? Hello?"

At the table sat a young woman, sobbing uncontrollably.

"Whatever is the matter?" asked the gentleman.

"The tiger is the matter," she said. "He comes by night. He ate my father, my mother, my sister, my brother. Tonight he'll eat me."

"Oh no, he won't," said the gentleman. "My friends and I will take care of that tiger." With that, he called in the hitchhikers in his horse's mane.

"May beetle, wait in that corner. When the tiger rushes in, put out the candle flame.

"Egg, bury yourself in the hearth ashes. When the tiger comes near, burst out at him so ashes singe his eyes.

"Crab, sit in the kitchen sink, and when the tiger goes to cool his burned eyes, gouge them out.

"Rice ladle, hide behind the kettle on the stove and when the tiger nears, slap him in the face.

"Awl, slide between the floorboards of the young lady's room and when the tiger passes, pierce his feet.

"Mortar, climb up onto the roof and when the tiger tries to flee, tumble down onto his head and crush it.

"Straw mat and pack-carrier, you hide in the storage area, and when the tiger is out cold, you'll wrap him up and carry him away.

"So, my friends, we are ready."

The young gentleman turned to the young woman. But she didn't need instructions. She picked up the candle and went into her room. The gentleman took his horse and waited in the stable.

Evening fell, and the tiger came down the mountain, teeth gleaming in the moonlight. He went into the house, where the candle flame drew him straight to the young woman's room. As he entered the room, the may beetle flapped its wings fast and the room went black.

"What happened to the candle?" called the tiger. "Where are you, Girl?"

"If you need light," said the young woman, "you'll have to blow on the hearth, to make it flame up."

SIBERIAN TIGERS
Siberian tigers used to roam the Korean Peninsula as recently as a century ago. But they were hunted out of the area. Today just over 500 Siberian tigers are alive in all of Asia. In 2018 South Korea opened a tiger forest in Baekdudaegan National Arboretum as a way to help save Siberian tigers from extinction. Tigers have acute hearing. So even though he couldn't see her in the dark, this tiger could have pounced on the young woman as soon as she spoke and revealed her position in the room. But in fact, tigers rarely prey on humans, so the tiger in this story is as unlikely as the other talking animals and objects.

The tiger blew on the hearth. The egg immediately popped up and ashes flew in the tiger's eyes. Screeching in pain, the tiger raced to the sink to douse his face. The crab gouged out his eyes. The tiger swirled around, blind and confused. The rice ladle slapped his face hard.

"Help," cried the tiger.

"This way," called the young woman.

The tiger ran into the young woman's room again and the awl pierced his paw. Yowling, he fell out the door. Down from the roof leaped the mortar, onto the tiger's skull. That was the end of the hateful tiger.

The straw mat wrapped itself around the limp corpse. The pack-carrier hauled it off to the river and dumped it into the current.

The young gentleman turned to the young woman. "You were brave and clever."

"No more than you," she said.

So they married and lived together happily with the may beetle, the egg, the crab, the rice ladle, the awl, the mortar, the straw mat, and the pack-carrier for the rest of their lives.

Bunbuku the Teakettle

junk dealer and the badger Bunbuku were friends. This turned out to be very good for the junk dealer, as we will see.

The junk dealer worked hard, but he made barely any money. People don't pay much for junk, after all. Even still, he shared his rice cakes and tea with the badger Bunbuku and tried not to feel too hungry.

Bunbuku watched people with interest. The priest had a round belly. The junk dealer had a flat belly. It didn't seem quite fair.

Now, Bunbuku was a magic badger. So he said to the junk dealer, "I'll turn into a teakettle. You can sell me to the round-bellied priest. You'll make enough money to eat well. At least for a while."

"But who wants to be a teakettle?" said the junk dealer.

The badger didn't bother to answer. People always asked pointless questions. He promptly curled himself into a teakettle.

The junk dealer wrapped the teakettle in an old flowered *furoshiki* and threw it over his shoulder. When he arrived at the temple, he untied the cloth and set the teakettle in the center.

"What a fine teakettle," said the priest.

"Yes." The junk dealer touched the teakettle lovingly. "Very rare. He tells good jokes. I call him Bunbuku."

"Bunbuku—a happy name!"

It was true: *Bunbuku* means "good luck." The junk dealer sighed. "We've shared many a happy cup of tea."

"I love tea. I will buy this teakettle from you. How much do you want for it?"

The junk dealer swallowed the lump in his throat. "It would feel strange to sell a friend."

"Here's a ryō. That makes it less strange. No? Well, how about two ryō? Ah, still with a long face? All right, three ryō, but that's plenty. Even for a friend. I'll treat him well."

The junk dealer went home. He put the money in a jar and sat down to drink tea. It was sad not to have his friend Bunbuku to share it. He wondered how Bunbuku was faring right now.

The priest lost no time. He sent his novice down to the river to scour the new teakettle with sand. "This will polish up nicely. Make it shine."

The novice scoured hard.

"It hurts!" cried the teakettle.

The novice ran to the priest and told what had happened.

"How strange. Well, all right. Just fill it with water and set it on the fire, then. I can't wait to taste the happy tea it makes."

The novice built a fire and set the teakettle over it.

"It hurts!" cried the teakettle.

The novice ran and told the priest.

"What can it expect?" said the priest. "It's a teakettle. Teakettles are made to sit on fire."

The fire burned higher and hotter.

A tail appeared on the kettle, then a face and feet and, boom, a whole bushy badger ran around the floor, screaming, "Hot, hot, hot. You burned my footsies."

The priest ran after the badger, but the instant he caught it, it turned back into a teakettle. "A bewitched teakettle! I can't have such a thing in my temple, no matter what kind of tea it makes." So he wrapped it up and carried it to the junk dealer. "I have a kettle to sell you."

The junk dealer stared in surprise. Then he shook his head. "It would feel strange to buy a friend."

"Nonsense," said the priest. "You sold it to me."

"And look how that turned out," said the junk dealer.

The priest was hopping mad. But what could he do? He left the kettle. "Good riddance."

The junk dealer put the teakettle gently on his table.

Bunbuku quickly turned back into himself.

"I missed you," said the junk dealer. "I have three ryō. Shall we go buy a nice dinner?"

"I'm happy with simple rice cakes," said Bunbuku. "But you can buy a nice dinner for yourself. Tonight and every night from now on."

"Three ryō won't last forever," said the junk dealer.

"I'll make you much more money," said Bunbuku.

"As a teakettle?"

"Don't be absurd. Who wants to be a teakettle? I'll do tricks and people will pay to watch me. Wait till you see me walk a tightrope."

So that's what happened. And it was all the badger's idea.

BADGERS
This is one of many Japanese stories in which an animal is translated as "badger" in English, but the characteristics of the animals with this label in the different stories vary quite a bit. So not all the stories are necessarily about badgers, but might be about some of the less well known animals of Japan, such as the *tanuki*, or raccoon dog. The true badger native to Japan, pictured here, is found on the three southernmost main islands but not on the large northern island of Hokkaido. Scientists think that this badger arrived in Japan via Korea. Its facial stripes are less distinctive than badgers in other parts of Asia.

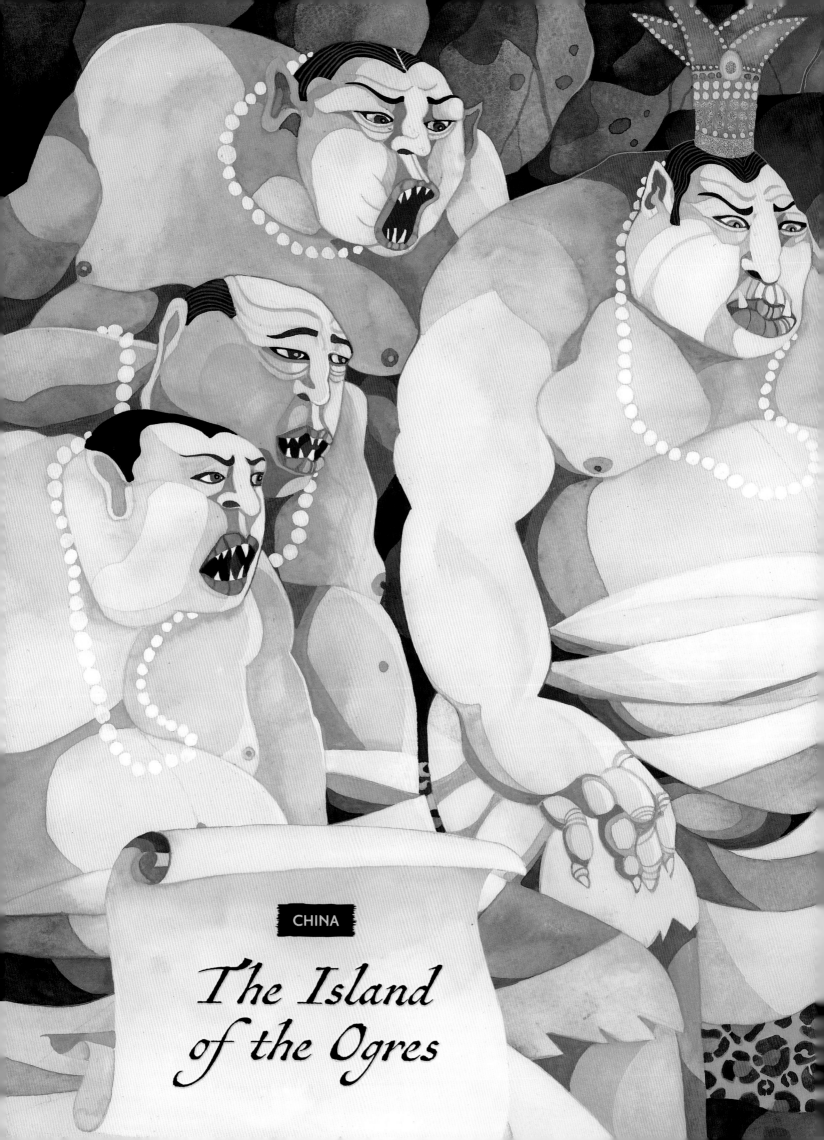

CHINA

*The Island
of the Ogres*

u was a sailor from the land of Annam in the Middle Kingdom. One day a storm pushed his boat to an unknown coast. The land was forested, but Su made out what might be houses up on a hill. He put food in his satchel and went ashore. He climbed up to a row of caves so regularly placed and sized, they could have been cells of a beehive. He peeked into one.

Two enormous ogres squatted together, devouring a deer. Their teeth were spears. Su ran, but the ogres' fiery eyes had seen him. They caught him and drooled, ready to eat him. Su opened his satchel and held out dried meat and bread. The ogres gulped it down. They grabbed the satchel and searched for more.

"It's empty," said Su. "But on my boat, I have pots and herbs and oils. I could cook you even better food."

The ogres looked at him as though he was a squawking bird. They didn't know human language, that much was clear. Su gestured building a fire and cooking. The ogres stared. Su gestured eating and rubbing his tummy. The ogres grinned. Hurrah! They understood. They followed him to his boat and watched him gather what he needed. Then Su and both ogres carried the lot to the cave. They built a fire, and Su cooked the remains of the deer.

The ogres devoured it. They licked their fingers. They danced in joy.

The ogres left Su and rolled a rock in front of the cave opening. Su sat alone in the dark, afraid. Then he felt around. There was nothing in the cave. The ogres must have hunted with their bare hands, eaten everything raw, and slept on the rock floor.

At last, the rock rolled away. One ogre carried in a deer. The other ogre carried in firewood. Ha! They wanted him to cook more food. Su handed one ogre a pot and gestured that he should fetch water. Su skinned the deer, cut it into pieces, and put the pieces in the remaining pots with herbs. When the first ogre returned with a pot of water,

Su poured water over the meat in each pot and set them to simmering. Soon wonderful aromas clouded the cave.

In came a whole herd of ogres: nine in all! They sat in a circle. Su placed the pots in front of them. The ogres downed that meat fast. They hooted and chortled and spoke their ogre language excitedly.

After that, the ogres brought Su more to cook: deer, wolves, and antelope. Somehow, they produced a giant pot, so he could cook for all of them in just one pot. They invited him to eat with them.

After a few weeks, the ogres grew complacent; they allowed Su to wander outside the cave. He followed them and listened closely as they made grunts and coos, calls and whoops, and strange words. He mimicked them. Soon he sounded pretty much like them. Su's behavior delighted the ogres. They said they'd never known a human who liked ogres. One woman ogre took his hand with a shy look. The others nodded happily. Oh! She was to be his wife!

Su was taken aback. Ogres ate humans. Even though they were nice to him now, what if he made a mistake and angered them? How could he trust an ogre wife? Plus, he didn't like the idea that the ogres didn't have names. They had a name for the island—Wo-Me—but not for each other. What was he to call his wife?

Still, this woman ogre gathered forest fruits for him. And she smiled a lot. And she liked the food he cooked. She showed him her favorite trees, her favorite cliff at sunset, her favorite beach with sand so silky soft it left your hand

tingling. In this way, they gradually fell in love.

One day, the ogres came into Su and his wife's cave wearing pearl necklaces.

"You look splendid," said Su, in perfect ogre talk.

The ogres beamed and told Su to prepare extra food today. Su's wife explained. "Today is the high festival. The king is coming to a banquet that you are preparing." She turned to the other ogres. "But my husband has no necklace."

The ogres each took five pearls from their own necklaces and gave them to Su. Then his wife added 10 from her necklace. She put all 50 pearls on a string around Su's neck. Never had he owned something so valuable. He couldn't stop smiling as he cooked the banquet.

When everything was ready, the 10 of them (including Su) marched across the ridge of the hill to a far cave. It was filled with many ogres Su had never met before. Everyone took a seat on rocks. The seat of honor was covered with leopard skin. The rocks circled a big stone table. That's where Su's herd put the banquet pots.

A gust of wind swept through the cave, and a gigantic ogre appeared, with eyes like dinner plates. The king!

The king looked right at Su. "Who's that fellow?"

"My husband," said Su's wife. "He prepared today's banquet."

The king took a taste. Then another. Then everyone was eating greedily. "From now on, you will cook every banquet," declared the king to Su. "But why is your necklace so short?" The king took 10 pearls from his necklace and Su's wife threaded them onto Su's necklace. Then in a blast of wind, the king was gone.

Over the years, Su's family grew. He now had two sons and a daughter. All had human form. All spoke ogre-talk, but Su also taught them human language. They grew strong and ran through the hills carefree.

One day Su's wife took their daughter and younger son on an errand. The north wind rose, and from nowhere came a longing within Su for his old home. On impulse, he took his older son to the shore, climbed aboard his old boat, and sailed away. It took a day and a half for them to arrive back in Annam. Su sold two pearls from his necklace, and the money he received was enough to buy a large home.

Su wanted to bring the rest of his family here. But he knew the people of Annam would never accept an ogre. His children looked like humans. But his wife did not. Oh, his wife would be miserable if she moved here. And Su didn't want to give up human life again, especially since his older son was doing well in Annam.

CHINESE SAILING VESSELS
From around III B.C.E. to around
C.E. 980, Annam was the name
of a region of Southeast Asia that
was under Chinese rule. This was
a period of Chinese exploration
of the world by both land and sea.
In fact, the Chinese invented the
stern rudder, which was far better
at steering a boat than poles or
oars. The sailboat in this story was
probably what was called a junk
in the West. Junks, which varied
greatly in size, were used mostly for
river transport, but they were also
seaworthy and used extensively for
trade between Chinese ports.

Su gave his older son the name Panther to use among humans. As a teen, Panther could lift a grown man with one arm. Panther was proud and he loved fighting. The top general of Annam heard of Panther's prowess and took him into the army. In a few years, Panther became a general.

Around that time, another sailor from Annam was caught in a storm and wound up anchoring off the Island of Wo-Me. A boy greeted him. "Are you from Annam?"

"Yes," said the sailor.

"Come with me." The boy led the sailor to a cave and fed him deer stew. "My father, Su, was also from Annam."

"Su!" said the sailor. "I know Su and his son Panther."

"When you see them next, give them my greetings."

"Don't be silly," said the sailor. "Greet them yourself. Come with me. Now. A good wind is blowing again."

"I love my mother and sister," said the boy. "I couldn't leave them."

The sailor sailed away and brought the message to Panther, the general.

Panther cried. Oh, how he missed the rest of his family. So he sailed off toward the island of Wo-Me. "Oh! That boy on the shore … that's my brother!" Panther steered the boat straight toward the boy. He jumped out and the brothers hugged.

"Where are our mother and sister?" asked Panther.

"I'll fetch them." Soon the younger brother returned with their mother and sister.

The reunion was tearful. "Please come back to Annam with me," begged Panther.

"They'll mock me because I'm an ogre," said the mother.

"No one will dare mock my mother. I'm a famous general."

The ogre mother missed her husband and older son so much, she decided to trust Panther's judgment. They all sailed to Annam. But as soon as people saw the ogre mother, they screamed and fled.

Once at Su's home, the ogre mother stared at her husband, her hands on her hips. "You should be ashamed. You didn't tell me you were leaving. We didn't know you were alive. You caused us misery." Su begged forgiveness, which she gave, because she did still love him, after all.

Panther's brother took the name of Leopard, and he loved hunting. Like his brother, Leopard became a soldier.

Panther's sister took the name of Ogrechild. Like her brothers, she was strong and an exceptional hunter. When she married, she rode into battle at her husband's side.

The ogre mother learned human language. She dressed in silk. She went by the human name Yóukè. Still, nearly everyone was afraid of her. Finally, like her daughter, she rode into battle, and because of her strength and bravery, no one could beat her. Soon the town trusted her. Her reputation as a warrior spread, and the emperor gave her a special title: Superwoman.

INDIA

The Four
Fairies

he Topaz Fairy, the Sapphire Fairy, the Ruby Fairy, and the Emerald Fairy were talented performers in the Heavenly Court of Indra. They sang, played music on their divine instruments, and danced light as butterflies. Indra was enthralled.

Until one day, Indra fell asleep during the Emerald Fairy's most intricate dance. The Emerald Fairy was aghast. She had worked so very hard to make this dance perfect. Indra didn't appreciate her at all.

Well, the Emerald Fairy knew someone who assuredly would appreciate her: Gulfam. Gulfam was a prince and, by all accounts, discerning. He could certainly judge fairy talents better than the awful Indra. The Emerald Fairy had seen Gulfam earlier that day on her way to the court, sleeping like a babe, but with the handsome features of an intelligent man. Though they had never met, she was instantly smitten. What she wanted now was to meet this Gulfam face-to-face, and find out if he was, in fact, as sweet as he was wise.

The Emerald Fairy wandered outside the palace, searching for Gulfam, when she came across Kala Dev, a powerful demon. "Kala Dev, you devil, you, please fetch Prince Gulfam for me."

Kala Dev didn't take orders from anyone—what was the point of being a demon if you had to take orders? But the Emerald Fairy used *please*. Plus green was his favorite color. So within a few breaths, he delivered Prince Gulfam to the Emerald Fairy.

"What's going on?" shouted Prince Gulfam, as he awakened in the strange garden. He jumped to his feet and his eyes alighted on the Emerald Fairy. "Who are you?"

"The Emerald Fairy. I brought you here. Or had you brought here. It doesn't really matter now, does it? You're here."

"You stole me?" Prince Gulfam put a hand to his temple, which was throbbing now. "You can't do that. It's wrong to go around snatching people."

"You're free to leave at any time. But you should know first that I, well, I have feelings for you."

Prince Gulfam blinked. "Do I know you?"

"I saw you sleeping this morning. You won my heart."

Prince Gulfam's cheeks went hot. "That's nice. But still, that doesn't make it right."

"Don't be angry. I need you."

Prince Gulfam put his hands on his hips and looked hard at the Emerald Fairy. His curiosity was piqued, he had to admit. "A proper apology might help right about now."

"All right, I should have asked you if you wanted to come. But something awful happened. I was dancing for someone and he fell asleep. Dreadful insult! You're wise. You can watch and tell me I dance well. Please."

"This is getting closer to an apology," said Prince Gulfam. "But you're not quite there yet."

"The someone I was dancing for is Indra."

"Indra? You dance in the Heavenly Court?"

"I do. And as apology for bringing you here without a formal invitation, I invite you to come see the four color fairies in a splendid performance."

"Humans aren't allowed in the Heavenly Court," said Prince Gulfam.

"I'll get you in. A prince as fine as you deserves such a treat."

Prince Gulfam's knees almost buckled. This fluttery creature with sparkles in her long hair and nearly transparent wings charmed him. She was downright darling, in fact. He was intrigued.

So Prince Gulfam snuck into the palace right behind the Emerald Fairy.

When the next performance began, Prince Gulfam watched from the shadows of the room. The Topaz Fairy played the sitar. The Sapphire Fairy recited poetry. The Ruby Fairy sang. All of them were wonderful. But the Emerald Fairy, oh my, the Emerald Fairy danced as soft as an evening breeze, as clean as spring water on the hottest day, as rhythmically as the prince's own heart. Indra had been a fool not to appreciate her. Prince Gulfam certainly did. Maybe he even loved her. Yes, he was sure he did. He sighed loudly.

"Who's that? An intruder in my court!"

Furious, Indra imprisoned Prince Gulfam in a deep, dank well. He snipped off the Emerald Fairy's glistening hair and clipped her gossamer wings and banished her.

THE MEANING OF COLORS
In this story the four fairies are named for gems of bright colors. Making colorful clothing is historically part of Indian society, rooted in the idea that cloth itself can have a transformative effect on the people who wear it. According to traditional beliefs, each color has a spirit that can combine with the moral fiber of the person who wears the cloth. Ruby, the color of blood and danger, signifies power. Orange-yellow topaz promotes natural fertility. Sapphire blue indicates wisdom. And emerald green reflects piety.

The Emerald Fairy wailed and wept. She wandered the world, ever more gaunt, sobbing for how unjustly her sweet love had been treated. She could no longer bring herself to dance, but she sang her sorrow eloquently, piercingly. People followed her through the streets, across the countryside, their heartstrings pulled by her keening. She came to be known for the beauty of her teary eyes and the haunting quality of her grief-stricken songs.

News of this enchanting singer finally traveled back to Indra. He had her fetched. Her woes had so transfigured her that Indra didn't recognize the Emerald Fairy.

The Emerald Fairy steadied herself. Indra had brought her disaster. And though she had broken his rule by sneaking Prince Gulfam into the Heavenly Court, that didn't justify the harsh punishment Indra had levied. So she sang her agony, she sang like she had never sung before, ending in a pool of tears.

Indra was moved to tears himself. "That song was a fine gift, worthy of a gift in return. What can I give you, lovely lady of sorrow? What does your heart most desire?"

The Emerald Fairy had hardly dared to hope. But now her words came strong and clear. "There is a human in your well. Free him, to be with me."

And so the Emerald Fairy and Prince Gulfam were finally reunited. What she needed to tell him about her wanderings and what he needed to tell her about his sufferings in the well—all that could wait. For now, in this moment, having each other, loving each other, was all that mattered.

The Frog in the Rice Paddy

widow lived near a palace. Every day she went to rice paddies, cut down stalks, and tied them into bundles to dry. Then she ripped the grains from the stems and pounded the husks off in a stone mortar with a wooden post. The widow gave the white rice grains to the king. But she was allowed to keep the powder in the bottom of the mortar for herself. This was her food, and she liked it.

One day the king had his servants beat out a proclamation on their tom-toms: "Rakshasi Ogress has a jeweled golden rooster. Whoever brings me that rooster will get half my kingdom plus as many goods as an elephant can carry."

Now, this widow was no ordinary widow; she had a son who was a frog. And this frog was no ordinary frog; when he heard the proclamation, he took the midrib of a date-palm leaf and strung rice on it. Suddenly he transformed into a man in princely clothing. A horse appeared before him; he instantly mounted and rode off to a city.

When the king of this city heard a prince had arrived, he invited him to stay the night, gave him food and drink, and asked, "Where are you off to?"

"To fetch the golden rooster and win the reward," said the frog-prince.

"You may need help," said the king. He handed the frog-prince a lump of charcoal. "Should it be hard to escape from the ogress, throw down this charcoal lump and tell it to form a fire wall."

In the morning the frog-prince traveled to the next city, where that king sheltered him for the night, gave him food and drink, and asked, "Where are you off to?" When he heard the frog-prince's answer, he offered a stone. "Should it be hard to escape, throw down this stone and tell it to form a mountain."

The next morning the frog-prince traveled to a third city, enjoyed a good night's sleep and food and drink, and answered the third king's question. This king gave him a thorn and said, "Should it be hard to escape, throw down this thorn and tell it to form a fence."

On the third morning the frog-prince arrived at the ogress's home. The ogress's daughter looked him up and down and said, "Where are you off to?"

"I've arrived," said the frog-prince. "Give me the jeweled golden rooster."

"I can't do that today," said the girl. "But I can tomorrow. Right now, though, come inside and hide before my mother returns and eats you."

The frog-prince followed the girl inside. She opened a trunk, in which there was another trunk, in which there was yet another trunk. In fact, there were seven trunks in all. The frog-prince didn't give a second thought to why this girl might be helping him—he still had pretty much a frog brain. He climbed into the smallest trunk and the ogress's daughter closed all seven trunks.

The ogress came home. "Whose horse is that outside?"

"It appeared out of the jungle," answered the daughter. "So I rode it home."

That night the ogress's nose wiggled. "I smell the sweet smell of a human."

"Of course," said the daughter. "You are always eating humans. The house reeks of them."

Satisfied, the ogress fell asleep. In the morning she left to hunt humans. The daughter opened the trunks and the frog-prince stepped out. "Take the golden rooster. But first, tie me up. After you leave, I will call out to my mother. She'll come at my third call. It will take her a while to untie me, so you'll have time to escape."

The frog-prince tied up the girl. Then he bounded away on his horse with the golden rooster under his arm. The girl cried out. At her third call, the ogress came running and untied her. "Who did this?

And—worse yet!—who took my rooster?"

"I don't know," said the girl, which was technically true. She'd never asked the frog-prince's name.

The ogress and her daughter set off after the frog-prince. Both their mouths drooled, eager to eat him. Are you surprised? Aghast? You shouldn't be. You see, the daughter was an ogress-in-training. She'd been good to the frog-prince for as long as she could bear it, but an ogress, even one in training, has to do what an ogress has to do.

The frog-prince looked back. They were gaining on him. He threw down the thorn. "Form a fence!" And the thorn transformed into a thorn fence. The ogress and her daughter called out, "No! Ouch!" They spent an hour climbing over it.

Soon they were gaining on him again. The frog-prince threw down the stone. "Form a mountain!" The stone transformed into a mountain. The ogress and her daughter spent another hour climbing over it.

Oh no! There they were, at his heels once more. The frog-prince threw down the charcoal lump. "Form a fire wall!" And the piece of charcoal flamed into a wall of fire that roared so loud, the frog-prince couldn't hear the screams of the ogress and her daughter. They burned to a crisp.

The frog-prince arrived back home. He went to the date palm where he had left a string of rice and ate all of it. In a flash, he was totally frog again. Good! That brief excursion into a prince's body was fun, but it didn't really suit him. Human food was awful. And what would he do with half the kingdom and all the goods an elephant could carry? He set the rooster on the horse's back and waved goodbye. And he returned to his ordinary—but wet and yummy—froggy life in the rice paddies with his mother.

THE IMPORTANCE OF FROGS
Rice paddies around the world are homes to frogs, and for thousands of years people have been hunting frogs there for food. But it is only recently that frogs have been recognized as welcome inhabitants to rice paddies for other reasons. These paddies teem with beetles, grasshoppers, and other insects that are crop pests. Mosquitoes also thrive in rice paddies, and they carry malaria and other diseases humans are susceptible to. Frogs eat a wide range of these creatures, so rice farmers today recognize frogs as an important part of the rice paddy ecosystem.

THAILAND

Princess Golden Flower

ong ago King Sanuraj of Thailand had a favorite wife who gave birth to a daughter.

The royal astrologer foretold the princess's future. "This child will give you much joy, but …"

"Yes … tell me more," said the king.

"She will have … a strange way about her. However, this oddity will save her life."

"Save her life? You mean she'll be in danger? Dreadful! We must keep close watch so this prophecy never comes true."

From then on, the princess was always accompanied by many handmaids. At first the princess seemed ordinary, with no strange ways. She didn't throw tantrums or suck on the tips of her hair or forget to bow. She was everything her parents had hoped for. Up until the time she uttered her first words. With each word, a golden flower fluttered from her lips. When she sang, golden petals swirled in a cloud around her. When she called her cat to come play, golden petals billowed out.

The king named the princess Phikool Thong—Golden Flower.

Every year, after the rainy season when the rice fields were plowed, the kingdom celebrated a festival of thanks to the Buddhist priests. Princess Golden Flower was the one to present those priests with new robes, the color of the flowers that fell from her lips.

At the new year festival, Princess Golden Flower had the honor of splashing blessed water on her mother's and the king's hands to purify them and show respect.

During the floating lantern festival, Princess Golden Flower and her friends built a boat of banana leaves and filled it with incense and lighted candles. They set the boat in the river, with a prayer to the Mother Goddess of the Sea to carry away all troubles.

In sum, Princess Golden Flower lived an exemplary life.

But one day, the princess, who was now a young woman, was bathing in the river with her handmaids when a vulture on the far bank ripped apart the carcass of a dog. "Hideous creature! Revolting stench!" Princess Golden Flower raced away. "I never want to see another vulture, never ever."

The vulture flew after the princess and her handmaids. "I am King of the Vultures, and you have insulted me—a fatal mistake."

The next day, the King of the Vultures turned himself into a handsome man and went to a cottage near the palace where an old couple lived. He gave them a box of jewels, and in return they were to tell King Sanuraj that he wanted to marry Princess Golden Flower.

The old couple obediently made the request to King Sanuraj.

What commoner dared to ask for his daughter in marriage! The king fumed. But he saw an opportunity to gain from this man's daring. "Tell him to build two bridges from your cottage to the palace gates. One must be gold, the other silver. He has 24 hours to complete this task. If he fails, he dies. If he succeeds, he can ask my daughter to marry him."

By morning two bridges spanned the space from the cottage to the palace gates, one gold, one silver.

The King of the Vultures, still in the form of a handsome man, asked the princess to marry him.

The princess blinked. This was her first marriage offer. It seemed the flowers that fell from her mouth put off others. So why not?

After the ceremony, they sailed away on her husband's ship. Princess Golden Flower asked her husband where they were going. He said nothing. She looked around at the crew. They just stared at her with one beady eye at a time. And, oh, that crew gave off a smell she recognized. A stench. Why, they were vultures in disguise!

When her husband went into his quarters and called the crew to join him, Princess Golden Flower stood on the deck and sang a prayer.

Mother Goddess of the Sea,

I'm your faithful,

　　please save me.

A SYMBOLIC COLOR
The majority of people in Thailand are Buddhist, and yellow is a color associated with Buddhism in important ways. For well over 2,000 years, Buddhist monks and nuns have made their robes from cloth dyed with the spices turmeric and saffron, and more recently, curry, cumin, and paprika—all of which give the cloth a color from orange to yellow. Yellow is also the color associated with royalty throughout much of Asia, including Thailand. Even the national flower of Thailand, the *ratchaphruek*, is yellow. Perhaps the flower that cascades from Princess Golden Flower's mouth is that very flower.

As she prayed, golden flowers flowed from her lips. She put one in a silver locket, set the locket in a coconut shell, and threw it into the sea, saying:

Noble person, noble soul
Find this shell,
    and keep me whole.

The voice of the Mother Goddess of the Sea called out:

Look up at winds where vultures ride,
Run now for cover,
    hide, hide, hide.

Princess Golden Flower looked up. The sky was full of vultures, including a huge one that was surely her husband. She dove under a barrel. The vultures alighted and hopped about the deck. They nearly tore the ship to bits in their search. Where had she vanished to? Finally, they flew off.

Princess Golden Flower crept out from under the barrel. The sea was calm as dreams. The sky was blue as hopes. And there, in the distance, was another ship. The princess waved her arms over her head and shouted. Golden flowers tumbled into the sea and floated to the new ship, circling it like a halo.

King Pichai, the ship's captain and the ruler of a nearby kingdom, scooped a coconut shell from the water. In it lay a locket holding a flower just like the flowers ringing his ship. "Hurry," he said to his crew. "Adventure calls."

One ship sailed toward the other as the sky darkened with a kettle of vultures, swooping this way and that. The King of the Vultures had returned for another search to find the princess. But King Pichai was a skilled sailor; within moments he boarded the vulture ship. As the King of the Vultures closed his claws around Princess Golden Flower's arm, King Pichai plunged his dagger into the giant bird's heart.

Princess Golden Flower watched King Pichai carefully. She half expected him to turn into some monstrous creature. "Are you truly human?"

"As human as you," said King Pichai. "Why was that vulture after you?"

"He wanted to punish me for insulting him."

"You must be a rash sort," said King Pichai. He smiled. "I kind of like that."

"Take me home, would you? On the way, we can talk."

And so Princess Golden Flower and King Pichai returned to King Sanuraj's palace, under the protection of the Mother Goddess of the Sea. In due course, they fell in love and married.

When the floating lantern festival came around again, King Pichai and Queen Golden Flower built a boat of banana leaves and filled it with incense and lighted candles, as well as thousands of flowers from the queen's lips. The banana boat carried their troubles away to the sea and they lived together happily, in the delicate perfume of golden flowers.

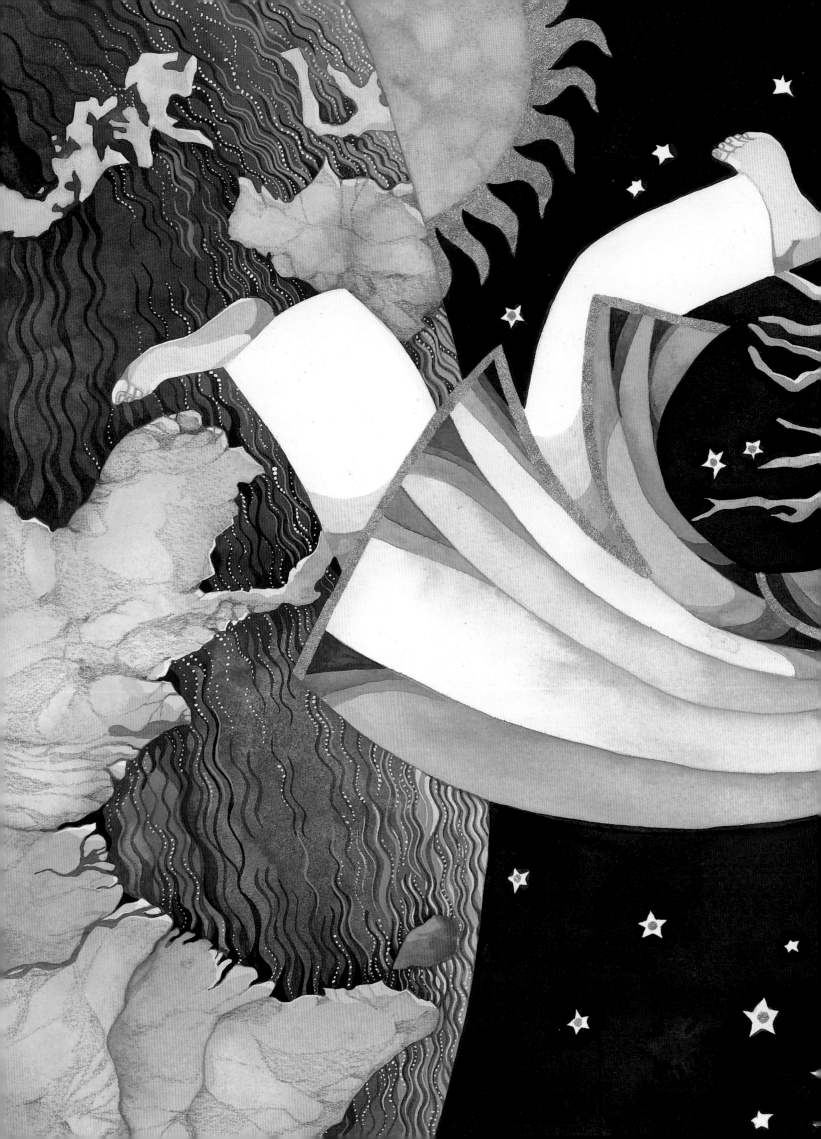

VIETNAM

The Buffalo Boy
and the
Banyan Tree

uoi's family was poor, really very, very poor, so he couldn't go to school. Instead, he worked for a rich farmer. Every day he looked after the farmer's water buffalo in the rice paddies. He prepared the slop for the hogs. He wandered through the forest collecting fallen dead branches for firewood. The work was solitary and exhausting. In return, the farmer fed Cuoi and clothed him and gave him a small amount of money to buy whatever else he might need.

One day Cuoi was carrying an armload of firewood from the forest when he came across a tiger cub. It was playing happily in the sun, leaping and rolling and spinning in circles. Cuoi was enchanted. This cub knew a joy Cuoi had never known. The boy dropped his firewood and picked up the little cub, to hug and tickle.

Only a moment later, a low, snarling growl came from the other side of a thicket. Cuoi couldn't believe how foolish he'd been. Anyone knew it was dangerous to play with a tiger cub. The mamma tiger would tear him apart now. He dropped the cub and ran for the nearest tree, climbing as fast as he could go.

The mamma tiger raced into the clearing and stopped, to stand over the cub's body. She nosed it. It didn't move! Alas! The cub had died when Cuoi panicked and dropped it. How horrible! Tears streamed down Cuoi's face. The poor cub, and the poor mamma. But he stayed silent in the tree, hoping against hope that the mamma tiger wouldn't discover him.

The tigress walked to the stream at the edge of the clearing and gathered banyan tree leaves in her mouth. She went back to the cub's body and chewed those leaves to a pulp. Then she spit the pulp on the cub's head. In less than a second, the cub jumped up and sprang about the mamma, showing no signs of having been hurt, much less dead.

Cuoi stayed in the tree a long time, awestruck by the magic he had witnessed. Finally, he climbed down and went to the banyan tree by the stream and collected its healing leaves. He headed home with an armful of leaves, instead of that armful of firewood.

On the way, he came across the body of a dog on the side of the road. Maybe the dog had chased a wagon and been run over by it. The wretched thing.

Cuoi put banyan leaves in his mouth and chewed as hard as he could until a soft pulp formed. He spit it on the dog's head, just like the tigress had spit it on her cub's head. In just a moment, the dog blinked, managed to stand on wobbly legs, and looked around, dazed. Then, in a burst of energy, the dog dashed off—as alive as Cuoi.

These leaves really could bring the dead back to life! Cuoi turned right around and went back to the tree. He worked all the rest of the day, digging it up, dragging it home, then replanting it in his family's yard.

"What are you doing, my son?" asked his mamma.

"This is a wondrous tree, Mamma. Treat it well. Never throw dirty water on it."

"What? Trees like dirty water."

"Not this one." Cuoi laughed. "This one is special. It might just fly off into the sky if you mess with it."

But Cuoi's mamma paid him no attention. If she had dirty water to throw out, she threw it on the tree. That made sense to her, after all.

The banyan tree, though, really was special. It pulled its own roots together as though it might yank itself out of the soil and go flying off—as if it had listened to Cuoi's joke and wanted to make it come true.

And amazingly, that's what happened! Cuoi was coming home from his chores at the farm when he saw the banyan tree float by as innocently as a cloud in a breeze.

He raced after it and grabbed hold of the roots. But Cuoi was skinny and small and the tree was thick and large. Cuoi couldn't anchor it to the earth. He couldn't even slow it down. Rather, he clung there as the tree carried him into the sky.

For days the tree floated with Cuoi dangling from its roots. Finally, it landed in a place unlike anything Cuoi had ever imagined. A barren place. Cuoi let go of the tree and looked around. Far off in space, he saw Earth. Why, he was on the Moon!

This was a horrible fate, to be all alone on the Moon. Cuoi sat down and tried to figure out a way to return home. But no solution came to him.

Instead, as time passed, Cuoi realized he didn't miss working for the rich farmer. It was nice to no longer guide the water buffalo through the rice paddies and get sore feet from trampling through the broken stalks. It was nice to no longer be knocked over by the hogs as they scrambled for their food. It was nice not to have his arms all scratched up from holding firewood. The only thing he truly missed was his family.

But wasn't that his parents, looking up at him right now? Cuoi smiled and waved as big as he could. He was sure they were smiling back, waving back.

Yes, this was a good life, this Moon life. This would do just fine. A buffalo boy could be a grand Moon boy. Why not?

So that's where he stayed, forevermore. On nights of a crescent Moon, children can see Cuoi up in the sky, sitting at the base of a banyan tree. He smiles and waves to them.

They wave back and sing:

Cuoi, Cuoi, buffalo boy, hog boy, firewood boy,
All alone on the Moon
No nasty chores, nothing but moonglow, stars, and sparkling joy
Dancing to your inner tune.

A SACRED TREE
Vietnam has frequent natural disasters in the form of earthquakes, floods, and tsunamis. The fact that people have to stay on the alert to such overwhelming displays of nature's powers may be reflected in the folk religions of Vietnam, which are founded largely on the natural world, including animals, mountains, and rivers. The banyan tree is considered one of those sacred entities and is often planted near temples. It is a source of peace. The story here is told (in many different versions) on the night of the Moon Festival, in early autumn.

INDONESIA

The Orphan Boy Who Became King

na Ilu was an orphan boy and Sumboli was a fisher who adopted him. They might have both been happy together; after all, each was alone without the other. But unfortunately, Sumboli was unhappy. And that's because Ana Ilu was lucky and Sumboli was not lucky, so the man grew more and more jealous of the boy.

Both of them set out fish traps every day. One day Sumboli found his fish trap totally empty. That was very bad news, because Sumboli was hungry. He checked Ana Ilu's fish trap. What! It was full to the brim with writhing, plump eels. That was just like Ana Ilu, to have such luck. Sumboli's stomach growled; he dumped all the eels into his own basket and brought the lot home and ate them. Later, when Ana Ilu checked his fish trap, there was a pig in it. A big fat pig. "Hale pig, what were you doing, out in the water like that?" But who cared really? A pig was a pig! "Goody!" Ana Ilu called out. He sold the pig at the market, used a bit of the money to buy a meal, then gave the rest away.

The next day, Sumboli's fish trap was empty again. So he wandered over and checked Ana Ilu's. Today it was brimming with perch, which Sumboli promptly stole. When Ana Ilu came by to check his fish trap, there was a deer in it. "Strong buck, why on earth were you swimming out here?" The foolish thing just looked at him. Well, a buck was a

A LAND OF MANY ISLANDS
Fish and rice are prominent in this story, as they are in the diets of many people in Indonesia. But that doesn't mean the society of Indonesia is homogeneous. Indonesia consists of many islands, of which around a thousand are populated, making it the largest island country in the world. Those islands are home to many different ethnic groups with varying cuisines. Some people eat meat (beef and goat, especially) and many are vegetarians. Some cultures also eat insects (mostly grasshoppers, crickets, and termites).

buck! "Goody, goody!" called out Ana Ilu. Another trip to the market, another nice meal, another sack of money to share.

On the third day, Sumboli found his fish trap empty and Ana Ilu's full of catfish. This was just too unfair! How long would Ana Ilu's streak of luck go on? Sumboli stole the fish, but in a moment of spite, he threw Ana Ilu's fish trap high up into a red lauan tree, where it got caught in the branches. That was not a smart move, for now no one could benefit from Ana Ilu's luck. But jealousy can make a person not think right. When Ana Ilu came to check his fish trap, it was missing. He looked every which way. There it was: high up in that tree. Ana Ilu climbed up with difficulty, and found his fish trap aflutter with laughingthrushes. He whistled to the birds and they whistled back. This was wonderful; everyone would want such a bird in their home. "Goody, goody, goody!" Ana Ilu enjoyed their lovely whistles all the way to the market, where they fetched a healthy sum—and more and more people were happy.

On the fourth day, you know what happened, of course: Sumboli's fish trap was empty and Ana Ilu's was full, this time of croakers. Sumboli stole those fish, of course, of course. And in his fury, he threw Ana Ilu's fish trap high into a waringin, a fig tree. Now, the waringin is a holy tree. So when Ana Ilu came along, he wasn't surprised to see a light glowing around his fish trap way up in the spreading branches. Holy trees were full of mysteries, after all. But when he climbed up and found a gentle girl in his trap, that did surprise him, so much so that he couldn't find the words to ask her how she'd come to be there. All he could think was how much better this was than anything before. A fine companion. *Goody—goody, goody, goody* filled his head.

"I am Ana Eo, the girl who lives in the sun." The girl smiled. "I'm the one who filled your fish trap with eels and perch and catfish and croakers. I filled it with a piggy and a buck and all those laughingthrushes. I've been watching you for years, bringing you what people call luck."

"But why?"

"I'm in love with you."

"But why?"

"Shouldn't we all love generous people? Besides, I like the way you say 'Goody.'"

"I thought that when I saw you. I thought, *Goody. Goody, goody, goody.*"

"I know." Ana Eo touched Ana Ilu's cheek. "I cannot come down to the ground with you, because I belong in the sky. But I will continue to bring you luck. Here." Ana Eo gave Ana Ilu a ring. "This ring's name is Sinchi Piranga. It will protect you."

Ana Ilu slipped on the ring and went home, bedazzled by the girl who lives in the sun. He could barely wait for the next day to visit her again.

Meanwhile Sumboli had been fretting all day. Jealousy had finally poisoned his mind thoroughly. That night he crept into Ana Ilu's room with a knife, ready to kill him. The magic ring, Sinchi Piranga, shone a magic ray, which killed Sumboli instantly.

The next day Ana Ilu visited Ana Eo in the holy fig tree again. The boy was baffled and saddened. He cried as he told her what had happened. He had never known that Sumboli wished him evil.

Ana Eo gave him a basket and a pan. "This basket will always be full of steamed rice. This pan will always hold as much fried fish as needed. Go now. Find a new life."

So Ana Ilu carried away the basket and the pan. Wherever he went, he fed everyone the best hot rice, the best hot fish. No one was hungry anymore. In gratitude, the people made Ana Ilu their king. And every night before he went to bed, he whispered up to the sky, just a single word: "Goody."

AUSTRALIA

The Bunyip

ong ago and far away, a group of men decided to set out from their home camp and go in search of food for their wives and children. Gathering food is serious business, of course, but these men were young, so they played as they went. They had contests to see who could throw a spear the farthest. Then they had contests to see who could throw a boomerang the best. Then they simply ran races. The sun beat down on them, but it didn't stop them in their games.

They came to a place that is a giant pool of water during the rain and flood season, but now, in summer, had only a few little pools here and there, with thick stands of bulrushes in them. "Bulrush roots are as good as onions," said one of them. "Let's gather them to take back to camp."

They pulled stems off a nearby willow tree and wove a big basket to carry the roots in. They were about to jump into the water and pull up bulrush roots when one of them pointed. "Wait! Look there! Eels. I've never seen eels in the daytime! It's almost like they came out to greet us. Let's catch eels instead."

Well, the others thought that was a fine idea. They made fishing lines from the bark of a nearby yellow mimosa tree. Then they put worms on their hooks for bait. But one of the men had saved a piece of raw meat from dinner, so he cut off a tiny bit and baited his line with that. He headed for the largest of the pools.

They fished for a long time. No luck. The sun sank lower in the sky. Still no luck. It felt like those eels had teased them, tricky creatures. Oh, it would be terrible to have to go home without even a basket of bulrush roots.

Suddenly, one line got a tug on it. It was the line with the little bit of meat for bait. The tug was so hard, the man could hardly keep from falling. He called to the others to help him. They all pulled and pulled, until the catch lay on the shore. It was some strange creature. Not a calf. Not a seal. All the men shuddered, for they knew what it was, though they had never seen one before: the cub of the awful bunyip.

The cub made a low, sad wail. From across the pool came an answering wail. The mother bunyip rose up out of her hidden den and screamed. Her yellow eyes burned with rage. She came at them.

"Let it go!" said the men.

"No," said the man whose fishing line had caught the cub. "It's my catch. I'm keeping it." He threw his spear at the mother to frighten her away. "I promised my sweetheart that I'd bring back food for a three-day feast. We can't eat this little bunyip, of course, but it will be a gift for my sweetheart's brothers and sisters. They'll love playing with it." The man hoisted the cub onto his shoulders and headed back toward camp.

The mother bunyip cried.

All the men left now. Sunset was nearing. The plain was all shadows, though light still played on the mountaintops. The men heard a rushing sound behind them. They turned and saw that the water from the bunyip's pool had risen. It had overflowed the banks.

"Why on earth?" the men asked each other. "There's been no rain. No clouds, even. This is odd. Worse than odd!"

They ran, panic in their hearts. When they got to the top of the closest mountain, they looked back to see if they were safe now. Horror! The pool had risen more than ever. The tops of only the very tallest trees now emerged from the waters. They ran faster than before, along the ridge connecting the mountaintops, all the way to their camp.

The man with the bunyip cub dropped it on the ground in the center of the crowd of old men and women and children. Everyone hushed, for they understood something terrible must be happening.

"It's the water," gasped one of the men. He could hardly catch his breath after all that running. "The water!"

He didn't have to explain, because they all could see the water rising to the mountain ridge now. The people clung to each other. What else could they do? There was no way to push back the oncoming flood.

The man who had caught the bunyip cub said to his sweetheart, "Let's climb that tree. The water will never reach us there." But already he felt the cold water. He looked down at his feet. They were webbed, like the feet of waterbirds! He looked at his sweetheart. She was girl no longer, but a big black bird! He turned to look at the other people, and all of them were birds, too. The man put his hands up to cover his face. No! He had no hands—he had wings. He tried to call for help, but the noise that came from his throat was unlike anything he'd ever heard before. It was like a bugle. And his throat, oh my, his throat was long and slender.

The water was all around him now, knee high, then waist high, then higher. The man found that he floated easily on this water. He looked at his reflection in the moonlit water: a swan!

The mother bunyip swam into camp and found her cub. And the waters subsided.

No one goes near the bunyip pool anymore, for fear of the mother's yellow eyes and strong jaws. Some say she has a den full of human treasures. But how could they know?

This was the one and only time that humans turned into swans. And the swan bevy they formed remains to this day unlike any other swans. That's because at night they talk a special language—they laugh and sing and tell jokes.

AUSTRALIA'S BLACK SWANS
There are several species of swans in the world, but the black swan is indigenous to Australia. Its bill is red and the tips of its wings are white (visible only in flight). Both parents share in rearing their cygnets, which are white with black bills until they mature. Black swans nearly always stay with their partner their whole life.

FIJI

Kumaku and the Giants

"Kumaku, fetch me water," called Kumaku's mother. "I've run out of salt. So it can't be sweet water from the spring. I need salty water from the sea. It's for cooking."

Kumaku was busy making herself a new garland of flowers. She loved how the pink and yellow flowers made a ring of spicy smell around her throat. That's why she made one every day, not just for ceremonies.

"Do you hear me, girl?"

"In a minute."

"Can't you be obedient just this once?"

Kumaku tucked a frangipani flower behind each ear. Unmarried girls were supposed to put flowers only behind their left ear, but Kumaku loved how they tickled her temples and she was little enough that she could ignore the scoldings people gave her. She set the rest of the flowers aside to work on later. "I'm ready."

"Good. And stay alert! There are dangers out there. Spiderwebs." Her mother shivered in fear. "You know what I'm talking about. Listen to me, please. But be quick. Hurry."

Kumaku took the coconut shell from her mother's hand and skipped past all the wood and straw huts, past the playing children, past the fresh spring.

The shortest route to the seashore went through the wilderness where spiderwebs hung from bush to bush. Kumaku stopped and stared at them a moment. Anyone foolish enough to get caught in a web would be eaten by one of the nasty giants that plagued the island of Rotuma. Kumaku had never seen a giant, but everyone talked about them.

REAL GIANTS
Fiji has many stories about giants, and some of them might be true. Paleontologists have discovered that Fiji was once home to a number of gigantic animals that today come in much smaller sizes. Among birds, one similar to a chicken weighed around 33 pounds (15 kg). By comparison, an ordinary chicken today weighs only around five pounds (less than 2.5 kg). A bird similar to a pigeon stood over three feet (1 m) tall. Today's pigeons are less than a foot (0.3 m) tall. The first humans to arrive in Fiji, around 3,000 years ago, found these giant birds easy prey for food, and over time these animals were hunted to extinction.

Still, Kumaku's mother wanted salty water, and she wanted it quick. Any other route would take much longer.

And most of all, Kumaku, little as she was, liked a challenge. Wouldn't it be fun to meet giants, so long as they didn't gobble her up?

Kumaku lightly touched the flowers behind her ears for luck and love. Then she headed straight for the sea, careful to pick her way past the spiderwebs. She swung her long black hair jauntily and sang as loud as she could, loud enough for any giant to hear:

> *I'm Kumaku, on my way*
> *to fetch water from the sea.*
> *Bula bula, welcome, giants.*
> *Come with big arms, come help me.*

Two giants popped out of the bushes. Real giants. With legs like tree trunks and eyes like the sun and snaggled hair. Kumaku hardly breathed as they lifted her high. She didn't dare wiggle. Her voice was trapped in her throat. Oh no! She'd finally disobeyed for the last time.

The giants carried her through the wilderness. They arrived at the sea and lowered her.

They were actually helping her! Well, this was wonderful after all! Her song had worked. Kumaku filled the coconut shell with water.

But what now? Their long giant claws curled around her.

Kumaku's heart felt like a wild bird caught in a cage. But she touched her flowers, for luck and love, once more, and she sang with all her strength:

> *Winds of Fiji, blow now blow,*
> *Swirl the black sands under the sea.*
> *Cast them in the giants' eyes*
> *So they cannot see this littlest me.*

Winds of Tonga, scream now scream,
Swirl the white sands of the sea.
Dazzle and bedazzle these giants' eyes
While I fly home fast as a bee.

The winds of Fiji blew, the winds of Tonga screamed. Black sand and white sand billowed from afar, they spun and twisted over the sea for hundreds of miles. They came relentlessly to the island of Rotuma, straight to the two giants that held little Kumaku. Those sandy winds burned the giants' eyes and scoured their skin and clogged their nose.

The giants flailed around and shrieked, miserable and helpless.

Kumaku fell free and her legs moved fast as wings. She flew through the wilderness, up the incline, past the fresh spring, past the playing children, past the wood and straw huts, all the way home. And the whole way she balanced that coconut shell full to the brim with salty water.

"Thank you, Kumaku," said Kumaku's mother. "You were very quick indeed. Thank you for being obedient just this once."

Little Kumaku smiled and went back to making her garland of flowers, just like before.

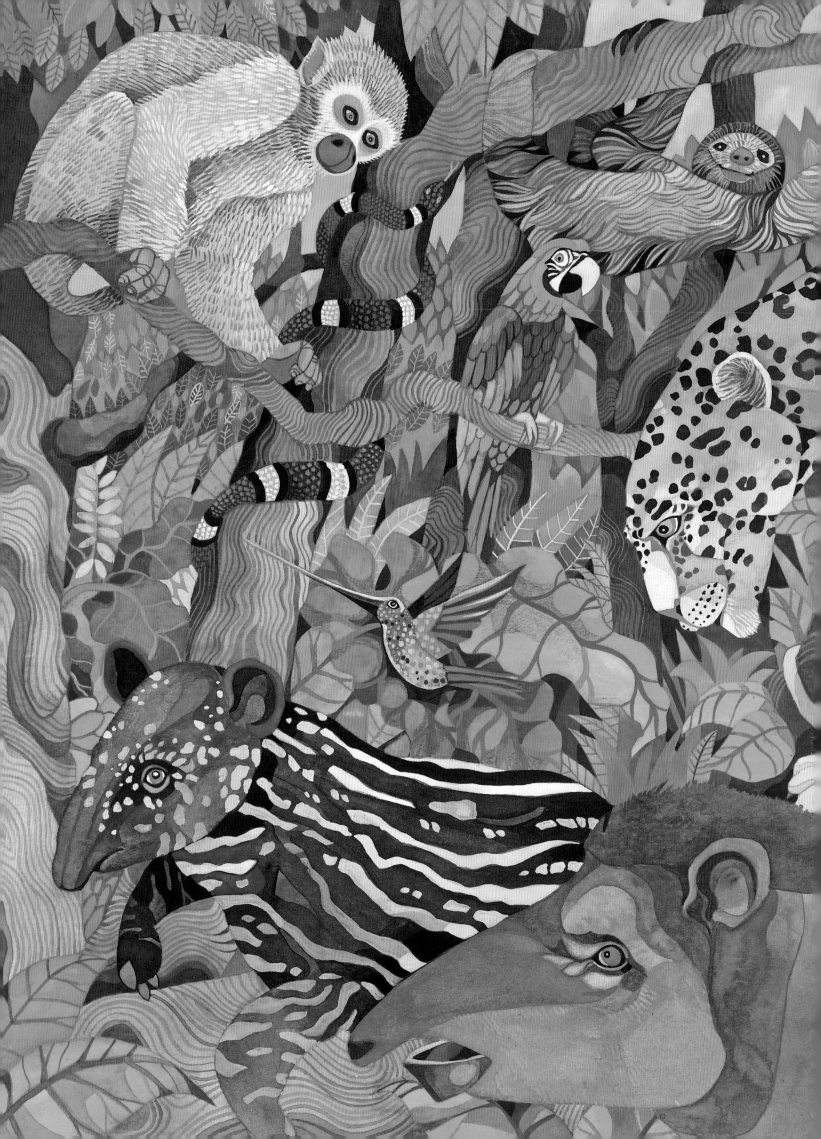

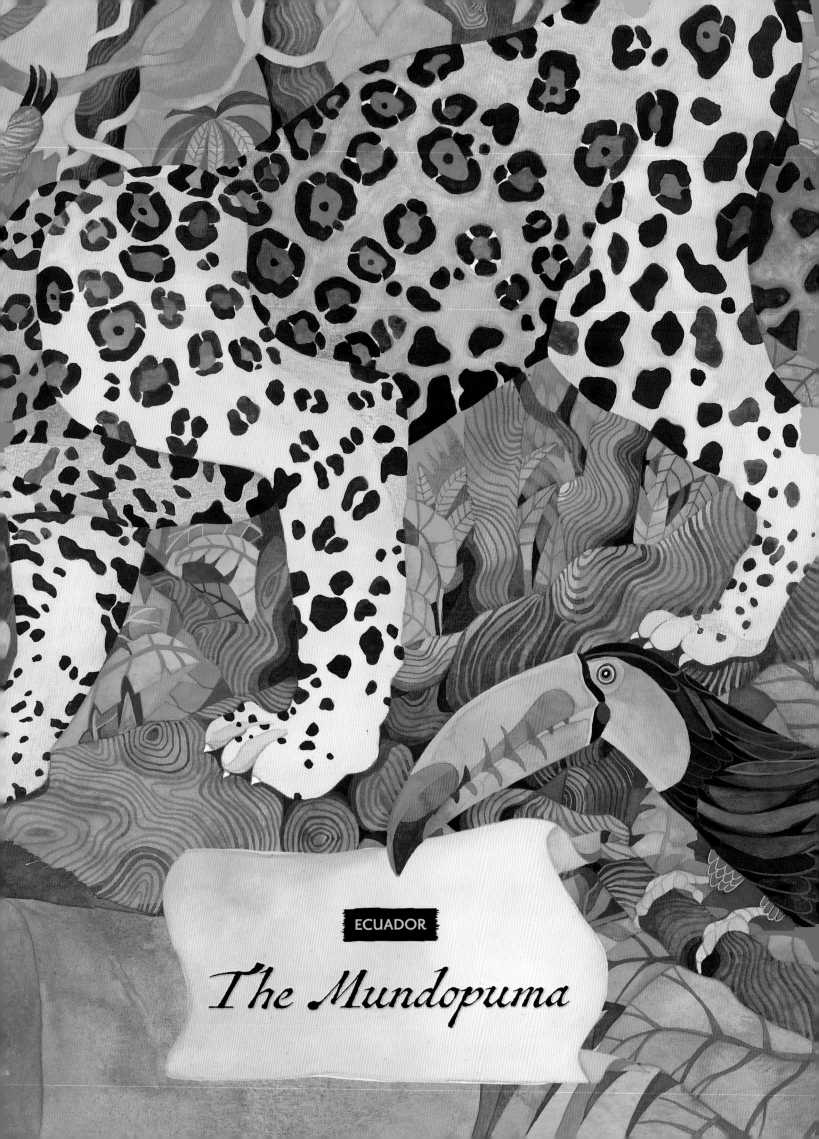

ECUADOR

The Mundopuma

Before there was time—
    Stop! Stop a moment and think of that.
    Look back—strain your eyes—
    so long ago your mind cannot fathom it.
    That's what I'm singing about—
    that time, there, then, the time before time.
The mother jaguar prowled the jungle.
    The great jaguar—Mundopuma.

Her crisscrossing foot trails made a pattern everywhere, everywhere.
    She raced through the underbrush
    at surprised deer, peccaries, tapirs.
    She climbed up the trees
    under astonished snakes, monkeys, sloths.
    She leapt into the waters
    upon unsuspecting fish, turtles, crocodiles.
    But that's not all she ate.
    She ate us! The people, the very old and the very young.
The mother jaguar hunted us with bloodthirst.
    The great jaguar—Mundopuma.

In the time before time, two brothers were born:
Dociru, then Cuillur.

     I sing of these smart boys, wise boys, beautiful children,
     who grew into smart men, wise men, beautiful humans.
     They lived near the mountain called Galera
     and they worked and worked
     and dug a huge cavern in the mountain.
All because they wanted to banish her.
     The great jaguar—Mundopuma.

They put a wonderful musical instrument in that cavern,
inside the mountain Galera.

     Then they called the mother jaguar,
         Come into the cavern.
         Come see our stupendous instrument.
         like the best organ in the world.
         Even we, with our pitiful human hands
         can make captivating music.
         But you, with your long claws,
         ah, you could do so much better.
And the mother jaguar watched and listened from afar,
for who doesn't love music?
     The great jaguar—Mundopuma.

First, the brother Dociru entered the cavern and played marvelously.
         Tiiiiiiin. Tiiiiiiin. Tiiiiiiin. Tiiiiiiin.
         Tiiiiiiin. Tiiiiiiin. Tiiiiiiin. Tiiiiiiin.
     Now the brother Cuillur entered the cavern
     and played equally marvelously:
         Tiiiiiiin. Tiiiiiiin. Tiiiiiiin. Tiiiiiiin.
         Tiiiiiiin. Tiiiiiiin. Tiiiiiiin. Tiiiiiiin.

The mother jaguar was stunned, enchanted, besotted.

The great jaguar—Mundopuma.

The mother jaguar said,

The music matters, it tugs at my heart,

but I know it's trickery.

You do it so easy

because you two brothers are special—wise.

The brothers called out loudly,

No.

We can barely play.

You have claws! You'll play much better than us.

Come in. Sit down on the nice chair.

Come play. Show us how it's done.

And the mother jaguar paced, drooling with temptation.

The great jaguar—Mundopuma.

The two brothers played again, better than before.

It's your turn, Mamma Mundopuma.

We'll listen from outside.

The brothers went outside.

And the jaguar, that strong mother, she went inside,

and sat down, and played.

A LEGENDARY WILD CAT

This story is about a jaguar, but she is called Mundopuma, which means "world puma" in Spanish. In some places the jaguar is called *el tigre*. But the jaguar is neither a puma nor a tiger. This powerful animal is a different species, and it is the largest wild cat found in the Americas. Jaguars were worshipped as divine in some ancient cultures of the Americas, whose art and architecture featured images of the big cats. Jaguars roam from South America all the way up to southwestern North America. Due to deforestation caused by logging and clearing for farms and ranching, however, the jaguar's habitat today is less than half what it once was.

The brothers called,

    That sounds so good,

    soooooooooo good.

  And they piled stones on the front and the back holes of the cave

  as the jaguar played.

Stones—the sounds of closure—*taasss taasss,* imprisoning her.

  The great jaguar—Mundopuma.

From outside the cave, no more music could be heard.

  Then came the feline howl,

  the roar, the screams of rage and frustration.

  The rocks of the mountain shivered and shook and tumbled.

  The brothers feared the whole mountain would crumble away.

  But in the end only one hole appeared, small and lonely.

The mother jaguar reached her paw through that hole

  and scraped at the mushrooms that grew there

  The great jaguar—Mundopuma.

These days the mountain Galera makes noises only sometimes.

  But when you hear them,

  you know this is the sorrow of the Mundopuma,

  the one who lives now only on mushrooms,

  chanting her pain, her loss, her defeat.

  But maybe, maybe, on the quietest of days,

  you can hear her playing that instrument.

The mother jaguar, who no longer hunts people,

  though some claim she escapes the mountain Galera,

    just now and then,

      to terrorize somewhere far from here.

      The great jaguar—Mundopuma.

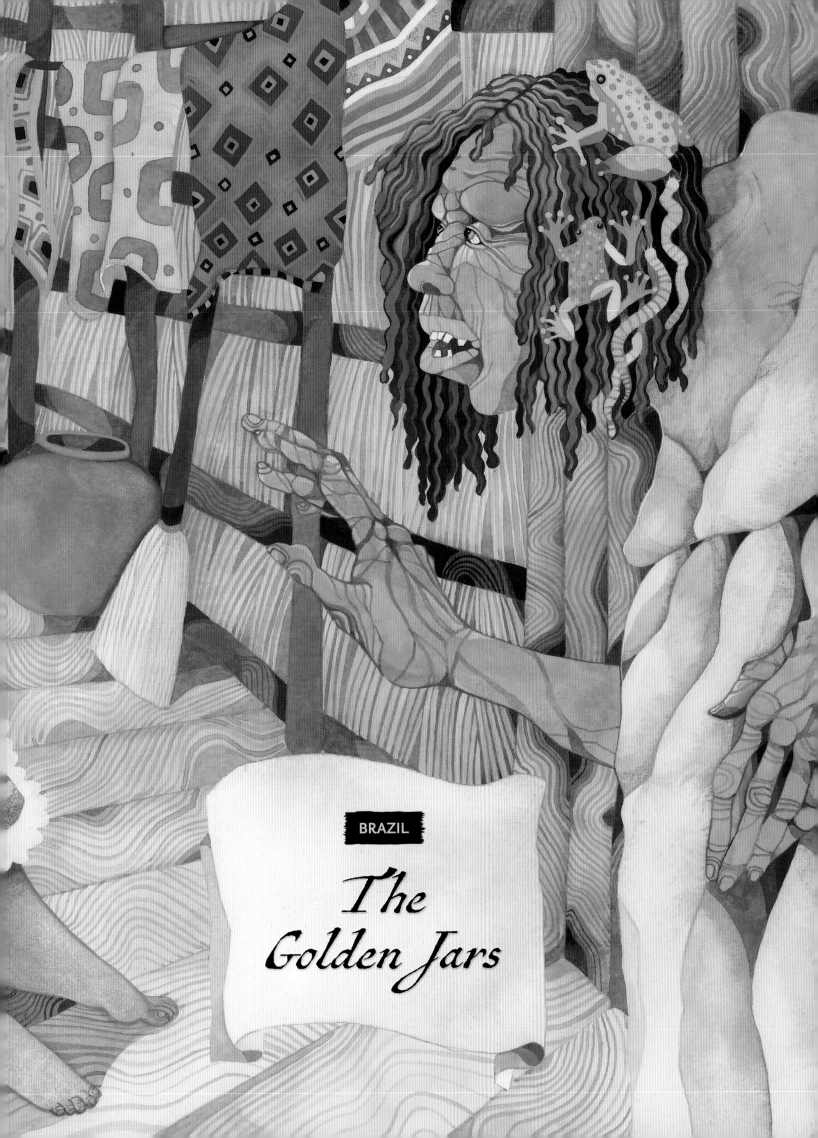

BRAZIL

The Golden Jars

 widow lived with two girls: her daughter from her first marriage and a stepdaughter from a second marriage. The woman detested her stepdaughter and made her do all the chores.

One day the mother and her daughter went out for a stroll and left the stepdaughter behind to scrub the laundry, clean the kitchen, and make dinner.

Knock, knock.

The girl opened the door to a skinny, ancient woman with a pipe in her mouth.

"My pipe went out. Please can you relight it for me?"

While the girl ran to get a hearth ember, the ancient woman dashed into the main room and grabbed a golden jar from the table.

The girl came back with the ember. The ancient woman was gone. And, oh no! Her stepmother had two beloved golden jars and one was missing. The ancient woman must have snatched it. Now the girl would be in deep trouble. She had to get the jar back.

The girl wandered, looking for traces of the old woman. What was that in the tree ahead? A golden bird? "Sunny bird, did you see an ancient woman pass holding a golden jar?"

"Are you mindless? Can't you see my leg is broken? Tend to it and I'll answer you."

The girl ripped cloth from the hem of her skirt and wrapped it around the bird's leg.

"Thanks. Now go ask the rabbit what you asked me."

The girl looked around. Was that a white rabbit in the thornbush ahead? "Milky rabbit, did you see an ancient woman pass holding a golden jar?"

"Are you mindless? Can't you see I'm stuck? Help me out and I'll answer you."

The girl tugged the rabbit free of the thorns.

"Thanks. Now go ask the cow what you asked me."

The cow? Where? The girl followed her nose, for cows are smelly. And there was a cow, tied to a tree. "Fragrant cow, did you see an ancient woman pass holding a golden jar?"

"Are you mindless? Can't you imagine how thirsty I am? Bring me water and I'll answer you."

The girl picked up a curved hunk of tree bark lying on the ground and went to the river. She used that bark as a bowl to fetch water for the cow.

Slurp, slurp, slurp. "Thanks," said the cow. "The ancient woman lives in a straw hut at the end of that road over there. She's not home now, so go in and wait for her. And while you're waiting, obey your heart."

The girl found the straw hut, went in, and waited, hopeful. She looked around. Dirty clothes everywhere. She lit a fire under the pot of water in the hearth, scrubbed the laundry, and hung it. And oh, the kitchen was a clutter of dirty dishes and slop on the floor. The girl washed the dishes, mopped the floor, and, as long as she was at it, mopped the floor of the entire hut. She found a basket of beans and vegetables in the corner. Under them was a bit of pork. The meat was drying out. How wasteful. The girl detested waste. She scrubbed those vegetables and chopped them and the meat, and she made a black bean stew, like her mamma who had died years ago had taught her. Now everything was just as it should be. She sat down and fell asleep.

The ancient woman came home. She nearly slipped, the floor was so clean. The aroma of black bean stew enveloped her. That girl she'd stolen the golden jar from slept in a chair. The warmth of pleasure surprised the ancient woman. But she wasn't about to let this girl know how she felt. She shook the girl awake. "Who do you think you are, bursting into a poor old woman's home and treating it as if it's your own? How will I ever find my things, now that you've stashed them here and there? And what's that in my pot? How do you know what I was planning to make with those beans and that pork?"

The girl bit her bottom lip and blinked at the ancient woman.

The ancient woman handed the girl a basket of string beans. "Make yourself useful. Get the strings off these beans."

The girl's fingers flew to the task.

As the ancient woman watched, pleasure came even warmer. "Now comb my hair. Just use your fingers, those quick fairy fingers."

The girl's fingers did their magic again. But slower now. The ancient woman's hair was full of worms and toads and spiders, all of which had to be gently plucked out and set aside, to slither and hop and crawl away. The girl smiled. It was fun to make order out of chaos.

"Thank you," said the ancient woman begrudgingly. "Have some stew." She watched the girl eat. "Now take this." The ancient woman handed the girl a length of twine with dried bean pods hanging from it. "This is payment for your stepmother's jar. When you need anything, pull off a bean and wish for it."

The girl accepted the gift. But she knew her stepmother would be furious. With each step homeward, the girl grew increasingly worried. When the girl's stepmother got angry, she turned ever meaner. Oh, if only the girl wasn't poor and didn't have to live with her stepmother.

The girl broke a bean from the twine and wished, "I want a rich palace."

A palace appeared in front of her. Huge and extravagant. Had she lost her mind? Could this really be happening?

The girl broke a second bean from the twine. "I want a carriage."

A carriage made of gold with crystal windows appeared in front of her. Six white horses pulled it. Lackeys stood by the side, in red velvet uniforms.

The girl was breathless. She broke off a third bean. "I want new clothes. The kind that someone who lived in that palace and rode in that carriage would wear."

She looked down at herself. She wore a silk gown. She touched
her head. A crown perched there. She took it off and, oh! Diamonds
studded it! Earrings hung from her ears. She took them off and rolled
them in her hands. Emeralds, matching the necklace on her chest. She
put the crown and earrings back on. Standing beside her, at the ready,
were ladies-in-waiting.

The girl entered the palace. Treasure boxes overflowed with gems
and gold coins. Closets burst with ornate gowns.

People from the village, curious about this new palace, came to
visit. The girl received them warmly and gave them gifts. Word spread
that the palace was inhabited by a beautiful, sweet princess. And that
word reached the ears of the girl's stepmother and stepsister. They
were greedy, and this princess was said to be generous, so they went
to visit her.

"What? Why, you're my stepdaughter," said the widow.

"How did all this happen?" asked her daughter. Her face pinched
with envy.

The girl told them everything.

The next day, the widow's daughter was at home when an ancient woman knocked on the door and begged for fire for her pipe. The greedy daughter determined to get some wishing beans, but without losing the second golden jar. So she threw a bucket at the ancient woman, then she ran into the kitchen to find pots to throw. The instant the daughter was out of the room, the ancient woman grabbed the remaining golden jar sitting on the table and vanished.

The greedy daughter ran down the road, asking everyone she passed if they'd seen an ancient woman pass holding a golden jar. When they didn't answer right away, she threw rocks at the bird, she yanked on the fur of the rabbit, and she whipped the cow. At the end of the road, she came upon the straw hut and burst in. She snooped about, breaking dishes, spilling food, putting out the fire.

When the ancient woman came home, the greedy daughter demanded she return the golden jar. The ancient woman looked at the mess the daughter had made of her home, but she smiled and gave the golden jar back to her.

"I want wishing beans, too," said the greedy daughter.

"I thought you might," said the ancient woman. She gave her a length of twine with dried bean pods hanging from it.

The greedy daughter rushed homeward, but as she got near, she thought about how envious she was of the new princess. Her mother must be envious, too. The daughter would be delighted if her mother was even more envious of her than of the new princess. A gigantic palace would do that, oh yes, one many times the size of the new princess's.

The greedy daughter broke off three beans at once. But before she could wish, she found herself in a cave, with only the barest bit of light.

A toad jumped on her. She screamed. Then a hundred toads jumped on her.

A snake twisted around her legs. She shrieked. Then a hundred snakes followed.

And spiders galore went running all over her, head to toe.

If she shouted for help, no one knew, because no one was close. Perhaps she's still in that cave.

The kind girl went about her life happy, unaware of what had happened to her stepsister. But her stepmother grieved at her daughter's disappearance, and the girl felt sorry for her. So the girl invited her stepmother to live in the palace with her.

The two of them lived there happily for the rest of their days.

DEADLY CREATURES
In this story, toads and snakes and spiders torment the greedy daughter when she finds herself in the cave. Brazil is famous for lethal dart frogs, but it is also home to small poisonous (but not lethal) toads. Brazil also has venomous snakes, several of which can be fatal to humans, including the golden lancehead viper. This deadly snake is so abundant on Brazil's Queimada Grande Island that it is illegal for people to go there. Finally, Brazil has some of the most toxic spiders on Earth, including the Brazilian wandering spider, which is often found on banana leaves.

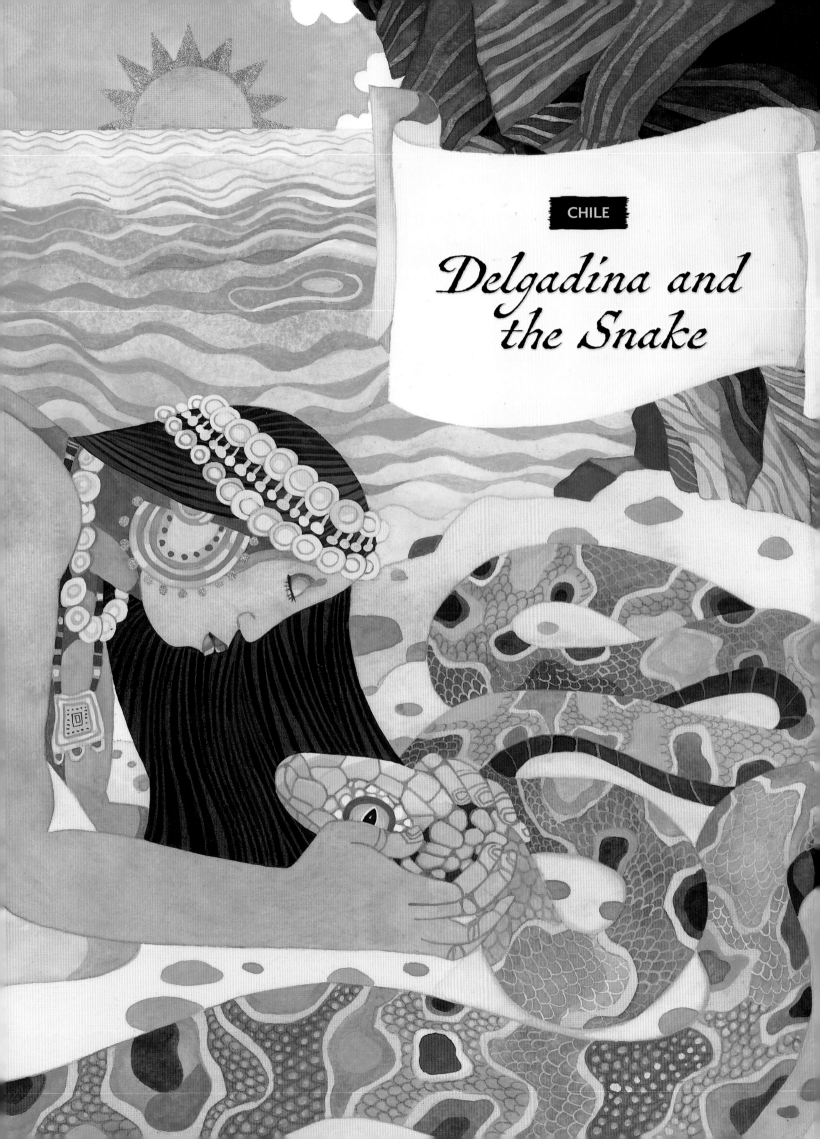

CHILE

Delgadina and the Snake

elgadina went to the stream one day to wash wheat for dinner. On the way home, a snake crossed her path. It was the length of her hand and bright yellow. Delgadina picked it up tenderly and carried it home.

"Yikes! Throw that dreadful thing out," said Delgadina's mother with a shudder.

Delgadina kissed the snake. "But it's darling!" She took a small clay pot and nestled the snake inside. They were poor, but whatever Delgadina had, she shared with the snake. Crumbs of bread. Sips of milk.

Months passed, and the snake grew. Delgadina moved him to a bigger pot. In a few months, she had to move him again, this time to a giant cask for storing wine.

Delgadina took the snake out to play every day. When Delgadina would make a special signal, the snake would crawl back into the cask. This was good, because the snake was now gigantic and Delgadina couldn't pick him up.

One day the snake said, "I'm too big for this cask. And I'm eating you out of house and home. So goodbye, dear girl. I have loved you."

Delgadina cried.

"Now, now, don't be sad. I'm giving you a treasure to remember me by. Rub your hands over my eyes until they drip with my tears. Good. From now on, whenever you wash your hands and shake them, gold coins will fall from them." The snake slithered away, calling, "Goodbye."

Had her snake lost his mind from living cooped up in the cask? But Delgadina put her hands in the basin of water she and her mother used for cleaning themselves, and shook them. Gold coins flew everywhere. Really? Or had she lost her mind, too? She dipped her hands back in and then shook them again. Yes! So many gold coins.

Delgadina soon grew accustomed to her new magic. She bought wonderful foods to share with her mother. She had a little cottage built, and she and her mother moved in.

The king got wind of the girl who could make gold coins by washing her hands and then shaking them. He wanted to marry her so she could make him richer. He asked an old witch to fetch the girl. Why he asked a witch, who knows? He may not have had the best judgment.

The witch knew Delgadina's mother, so she told her that the king wanted to see the girl.

"Heavens above!" cried Delgadina's mother. "Why?"

"I'll find out," said the witch, which was a sneaky thing to say, since the king had already told her he wanted to marry Delgadina. "Let me take her to the castle."

On the way to the castle, the witch plucked out Delgadina's eyes and threw her into the sea. Then she fetched her own daughter and brought her to the king. "Here's that girl who makes gold coins fly from her hands. She wants to marry you," she said, which was true: The witch's daughter thought marriage to a king would be grand.

The king did not find the witch's daughter charming. But money was money. "Okay, we'll marry tomorrow."

Meanwhile, poor Delgadina swam blindly in the sea. Fishermen found her and brought her back to the cave that was their home. They tended to her kindly.

Back at the castle, the king discovered that his new wife did not have a way with money after all. "What's the matter with you? You're supposed to make gold coins."

"I can't," said the witch's daughter. "I used to be able to. But once I married you, I lost that power. It's your fault."

The king believed her. He wasn't happy about being married to this unpleasant lass, but what could he do?

As for Delgadina, she remained in that cave. One day she was sitting all alone when she heard, "Delgadina! What are you doing in this cave?"

Delgadina recognized the voice instantly. "My beloved snake!"

"How did you wind up here?"

"A witch plucked out my eyes and threw me in the sea. Fishermen rescued me."

The snake wept. "Rub your hands over my eyes. All right now, open your own eyes."

And somehow Delgadina had eyes again. "Oh my beautiful snake! Thank you."

"Your eyes are deep sea green now. You look charming. Climb on my back and hug tight."

Delgadina rode the snake to the spot where the witch had tossed her into the sea.

"Walk home now," said the snake. "Don't dawdle. Straight home."

Delgadina stepped onto the shore. "Goodbye, sweet friend." She was so happy, she skipped home. When she burst in on her mother, the old woman gasped in shock. But Delgadina explained what had happened, and they sang and drank the traditional maté tea.

Delgadina, of course, went back to her old way of washing her hands, shaking them, and producing a spray of gold coins. That's how she supported herself and her mother, after all. Soon word got back to the king that the girl of the gold coins was once more with her mother. *Oh dear,* thought the king, *did I marry the wrong girl?* So he cooked up a plan. He invited everyone in the kingdom to a banquet at the palace.

After the meal, fingerbowls were put on the table. When Delgadina dipped her fingers and then shook them, gold coins sprinkled everywhere. The king quickly banished his former wife and her witch mother and asked Delgadina to marry him.

Delgadina smiled. "Mother and I are doing fine, just the two of us. But you can court me if you like, and we'll see what happens."

SNAKE SENSES

The snake in this story appears to have true affection for Delgadina and recognizes her years after having left her. In real life this is unlikely. Most snakes have poor eyesight. Instead of relying on sight, they negotiate the world through an excellent sense of smell and through heat detection. And snakes' ears are internal, making them sensitive to vibrations that come from the surfaces they slither on—but maybe not to sounds in the air. It would be very hard for a snake to recognize people—who are differentiated mostly by sight and sound and not so much by smell or temperature. Still, unlikely things can happen.

MEXICO

Red Cascades

wo waterfalls plunged from atop a majestic mountain. Their liquid ran red and gushed into swirling pools at the bottom. They seemed to be twin cascades. But they weren't. One flowed with wine; the other flowed with blood.

Naturally, these cascades were enchanted. If you bathed in the wine pool, you gained wisdom. Pilgrims came to bathe and grow wise and live forever after in peace. If you bathed in the blood one, you turned to stone. No one chose to visit that cascade. But many mistakenly did. The blood pool was surrounded by stones that were statues of those poor souls, but not a single one was recognizable. They simply looked like stones, worn down over time.

In the land of these two cascades lived a king and his daughter. The king encouraged her in every way. She grew up thinking she could do anything, anything at all. The king was happy. What a fine daughter. And besides her great confidence, she had cute little feet, and dainty little hands, and big apple cheeks. The king wanted everything in his daughter's life to be perfect. That required that he be wise.

"Prepare my horse," said the king to his servants. "I will go bathe in the wine cascade pool."

"Careful, my king," said the king's wizard. "The two cascades look alike. It's easy to be deceived and wind up turned to stone."

"I have decided to do this," said the king. "For my daughter. You will accompany me. Somehow we will make the right choice. Maybe we can even end the curse of the blood cascade."

The king's hopes became the gossip of the whole town. They even reached the ears of the princess.

"Where is the wine cascade?" asked the princess of her servant.

"I want to be wise, too."

"Don't be reckless, sweet princess. Beside
the wine cascade is a blood cascade. If even a drop
of the blood should get on you, you'd turn to stone."

"I'm not afraid. I can do anything. Prepare my horse."

The princess galloped away so fast, she arrived at the
cascades before her father. They were glorious. The liquids
shined like rubies. She jumped off her horse and dove into
the nearest pool. The transformation was so instantaneous
that the princess barely felt her blood go cold before she was
entirely stone.

Soon the king arrived. What was that? He slid off his
horse and walked slowly toward the statue. Let that stone
foot not be so small. Let that stone hand not be so graceful.
Let that stone cheek not be so full. Alas, the king could not
lie to himself. That statue was his daughter. And even as he
watched, the lines of her face disappeared, the outlines of
her arms disappeared, she was nothing but an unrecogniz-
able stone. The king crumpled to his knees and his eyes
made their own cascades. Finally, he mounted his horse
and returned home. His rash decision had somehow
killed his beloved child. Desires could be deadly. This
sad wisdom sat heavy on his chest.

Years passed and the blood cascade washed over
the statue of the princess, polishing her so
that she glowed. The beauty she had had as a
young girl was enhanced many times over.

One day a prince from a far land traveled through our king's land. This prince had heard about the enchanted cascades, but he didn't believe they existed. The prince just happened to pass by the twin cascades, however. When he saw the red statues, he realized the story of the enchanted cascades was true, after all. The prince said a prayer for the poor lost souls who had turned into statues. As he walked closer to the blood cascade, he saw a particularly dazzling ruby in the swirling pool. He fished it out with a stick. Once it was dry, he put it in his pocket.

Back at his own castle, the prince gave the ruby to the royal jewelers. "Make me an amulet, please."

The royal jewelers all exclaimed on the gem's beauty:

"Astonishingly brilliant!"

"Never have I seen such a perfect precious stone."

"And there's something else about it. Something special beyond the way it looks."

"Yes! Some kind of power. I don't understand, but I know it's there."

So the jewelers called in the royal wizard. The royal wizard examined the ruby, then turned to the prince. "You cannot make an amulet from this stone, for trapped inside it is a princess. She called to you, which is why you saw this particular stone in the bloody swirls."

The prince knew at once that this was true. The ruby was calling to him even now. "What should I do, Wizard? How can I free her?"

"Return to the enchanted cascades. Bathe this ruby in the waters of the wine cascade. The wisdom that flows over and around it will break the enchantment."

The prince returned to the land of the enchanted cascades. He bathed the ruby in the wine cascade. Gradually, the layers of stone washed away, and the prince found

GEMS AND JEWELRY
The precious stones known as rubies are the red variety of the mineral known as corundum. Blue corundum is called sapphire. The element chromium is what gives rubies their hue, from pink to many different shades of red. Mexico has a range of precious stones, including opals, agates, turquoise, jasper, and obsidian. The indigenous people of Mexico—including the Aztec and the Maya—were among the first in the world to adorn themselves with precious stones, a tradition that is still alive today.

himself holding the hand of a princess. She was soaked to the bone, and weary with the weight of years of being trapped, but she was beautiful, because the wine cascade had imbued her with wisdom. And that wisdom made the princess pull hard on the prince's hand, so that he fell into the pool of wisdom.

The prince and princess played in the pool and drank deeply. Then they went to the blood cascade and used sticks to fish out all the other stones. They washed them in the wine pool, and the poor souls trapped in the stones were once again alive and free.

"No one should turn to stone again," said the princess. So the princess and the prince and the many people they had freed climbed to the top of the majestic mountain and dammed up the headwaters of the blood cascade.

The princess led the prince back to her home. Her father was old now, but he recognized her immediately. With joy, he gave half his kingdom to the prince. The princess got the other half.

The prince and princess took a sensible amount of time to get to know one another. They were wise, after all, so they weren't about to rush into a relationship. With time, they realized they were, indeed, compatible. They loved each other. So they married and ruled the united kingdom with kindness—which is what wise rulers do.

Afraid of Nothing

our ghosts were hanging out in the way ghosts do—talking, laughing, smoking ghost smoke. It was a grand old time.

The first ghost said, "I know a young man who's not afraid of anything. Not even us."

The second ghost said, "Rubbish. I could scare him and make his heart race."

The third ghost said, "And I could make him shake with fear and hide like a baby."

The fourth ghost said, "How about a wager? The ghost who scares him the worst wins. We'll each give the winner our ghost horse."

And so it was agreed.

Soon enough The Man Who Was Afraid of Nothing came walking along at night under a bright moon. The first ghost popped up in his path, in the form of a skeleton. "*Hou*, friend." He clacked his teeth and sounded like a drum.

"*Hou*, cousin. Out of the way. I need to pass."

"First we'll play hoop and stick. The loser gets turned into a skeleton."

"You're already a skeleton," said The Man Who Was Afraid of Nothing. He laughed and bent the skeleton into a hoop, tied it firm with grass, and used one of the skeleton's leg bones as a stick to roll that hoop along. "Ha, ha! I won. Want to play shinny ball?" He smacked the skeleton's skull with that leg bone and sent it flying like a ball.

"*Oweeoweeowee!*" screamed the skull. "What a headache."

"Who wanted to play games in the first place?" said The Man Who Was Afraid of Nothing. He kicked the skull and walked on.

Now the second ghost popped up in his path, also in the form of a skeleton. The skeleton grabbed The Man Who Was Afraid of Nothing by the hands. "How about a dance, friend?"

"Sure, cousin. But we need the music of drums." The Man Who

Was Afraid of Nothing grabbed the skeleton's skull and tucked it under one arm. He grabbed the skeleton's thighbone and used it as a drumstick, beating it on that skull.

"*Oweeoweeowee!*" screamed the skull. "What a headache."

"Really? Ghosts don't feel pain."

"I do."

"You little whiner, you. You spoiled our dance." The Man Who Was Afraid of Nothing kicked the skull away and threw the rest of his bones after him.

"Rotten fellow!" screeched the skull. "It'll take me hours to put myself together again."

"You better start, then." And The Man Who Was Afraid of Nothing walked on.

Now the third ghost popped up in his path, once more in the form of a skeleton.

"What a bore you are," said The Man Who Was Afraid of Nothing. "Didn't I already meet you twice before?"

"Those were my cousins. They're nothing compared to me. Wrestle me. The loser gets turned into a skeleton."

"You're just like your cousins—brainless, all of you; you're already a skeleton. Besides, I don't feel like wrestling. I feel like sledding. Look at all this snow. Your rib cage isn't as good as a buffalo's, but it'll have to do as my sled." The Man Who Was Afraid of Nothing jumped on the skeleton's rib cage and slid down the hill. "Yay!" he shouted.

"Stop!" screamed the ghost's skull. "You'll break my ribs."

"Look how short you are without a rib cage," said The Man Who Was Afraid of Nothing. "That's funny." And he threw the rib cage into a stream.

"Oh no! I need my ribs," screamed the ghost's skull.

"Go dive in after them," said The Man Who Was Afraid of Nothing. "You could use a bath anyway, you dirty man skeleton."

"I'm a woman," said the ghost.

"Oops," said The Man Who Was Afraid of Nothing. "It's hard to tell with a pile of bones." And he walked on.

Now the fourth skeleton appeared. He was the chief of the ghosts, and he came in the form of a skeleton riding on a skeleton horse. "I'm going to kill you," he said.

"Bah!" The Man Who Was Afraid of Nothing made ugly faces. He showed his teeth and rolled his eyes and growled. "I'm a ghost, too, you know, and a far more terrible one than you are."

The chief ghost panicked. He tried to turn his horse away, but The Man Who Was Afraid of Nothing caught hold of the bridle. "Get off. This horse is mine now." The Man Who Was Afraid of Nothing yanked that ghost off his mount and broke it all to pieces. He climbed onto the skeleton horse and rode it into camp.

By now, dawn was breaking. Women on their way to fetch water saw The Man Who Was Afraid of Nothing on the horse skeleton. They shrieked in fear. All the other villagers peeked out of their teepees and then stayed inside, trembling.

But as the sun came out fully, the skeleton horse disappeared.

The Man Who Was Afraid of Nothing laughed and laughed. He told all the men how he had put those four ghosts to shame. Oh, were they in awe of him. Nothing scared that fellow.

"Hey," said one of the villagers. "Look at that tiny spider."

"What spider?" said The Man Who Was Afraid of Nothing.

"That one, crawling up your sleeve."

"Yikes!" screeched The Man Who Was Afraid of Nothing. "Get it off me. Fast. I hate spiders!" He shivered and shook.

A little girl picked the spider off him and laughed.

TINY DANGERS

This story pokes fun at a man who is unafraid of ghosts but terrified of spiders. In fact, nearly all spiders produce venom to kill their prey, though the venom of most spiders is not strong enough to kill a human. Plenty of other small creatures produce toxins potentially fatal to humans, though, including warm water cone snails, poison dart frogs, and the blue-ringed octopus, as well as microorganisms such as the rotavirus and a few kinds of bacteria. So the man in this story might well not be a fool.

CHEYENNE,
NORTH AMERICA

Eyeball Tricks

echo was a braggart and a buffoon, always trying to make people think he was important.

One day Vecho came across a medicine man who said, "Want to see a trick?" The medicine man shouted, "Eyeballs, fly out of my head and go dangle from that tree." In a flash, the medicine man's eyeballs shot out of his head and dangled from the tree.

Vecho stared. How on earth?

The medicine man shouted, "Eyeballs, come back where you belong." And they did.

"Wondrous trick!" Vecho walked in a circle. "Teach it to me. Give me just a speck of your power." That way when Vecho did the trick, everyone would think he was important. Yes!

"Why not?" said the medicine man. "But I warn you. You can do this trick at most four times a day. If you do it a fifth time, your eyeballs will never come back to you."

"I promise," said Vecho. He walked off, tingling with excitement. Had the medicine man really transferred even the teeniest bit of power to him? He went to a spot where no one could see him and said, "Eyeballs, fly out of my head and go sit on that ledge." All of a sudden, Vecho could see nothing! Gently, gently, he felt his face. Where his eyeballs used to be, there were gaping eye sockets. His heart hammered. "Eyeballs, come back where you belong." And they did. Yes, yes! He had the power!

Vecho walked on, alone. Up ahead was a tree. He had to try the trick again. After all, what if he'd been hallucinating? "Eyeballs, fly out of my head and go dangle from that tree." He went blind. Vecho snapped his fingers. "Get back here now, eyeballs!" And his eyeballs obeyed.

This was the best thing that had ever happened to Vecho. He was powerful. He was important. He did the trick two more times, to make sure he had mastered it.

Vecho wandered happily and came to a village with lots of people gathered together talking. "Guess what I can do," he said to the villagers. After all, they should know how important he was. They should marvel at him. "I can make my eyeballs fly out of my head and"—Vecho looked around—"and go dangle from that tree. And when I tell them to come back, they'll zip right back to me."

The villagers laughed at him. "Liar!"

"It's true!" Vecho stomped his feet in anger. "I have medicine man powers!"

"Prove it."

Vecho scratched his head. How many times had he done the trick today? His eyeballs had flown out of his head four times, he was pretty sure of that. But the first time … well, that couldn't really count … after all, it was just practice. So he was allowed one more time. "Eyeballs, fly out of my head and go dangle from that tree."

The eyeballs obeyed.

"Amazing!" shouted the people.

"What power!"

"He's a medicine man if ever there was one."

Vecho strutted proudly through the crowd, not even caring who he bumped into. Yes, yes, yes. He was everything he'd ever hoped to be. "Hey, eyeballs!" he shouted at last. "Come back where you belong."

But the eyeballs stayed in the tree, glistening in the sun, free as the air.

Vecho's throat constricted. His stomach felt sick. "Come back," he shouted. "Come back right now." Nothing changed. "Come back, you dirty eyeballs! I command you!" Nothing.

"Look at that crow," called someone.

Vecho heard the beat of wings.

"Good looking eyeballs," said the crow. "I might as well eat them." *Slip, slurp.* "Yum."

"Well, he wasn't much of a medicine man after

all, was he?" said a villager. Everyone laughed and walked away.

Vecho stumbled, hands outstretched. What now? He didn't know how to manage without his eyes. He walked without knowing where, into the cool of the forest, and he plopped down, landing on a stone. He dropped his head in his hands and cried.

Squeak. The sound of a mouse.

"Darling mousey," said Vecho. "Be kind. Lend me an eye so we can both see."

"My eyes are tiny," said the mouse. "What good would one of my eyes do you?"

"Please. It has to be better than nothing. Please, please."

Well this was a kind-hearted mouse, indeed, for he popped out an eye and gave it to Vecho.

The mouse had been right; his eye sloshed around in Vecho's eye socket. But Vecho could now see a speck of light. He stood and wandered out of the forest and into a field, where he met a buffalo.

"Brave buffalo," said Vecho. "Dear strong brother buffalo. I see next to nothing from my one tiny mouse eye. Be kind. Lend me an eye so we can both see well."

"My eyes are huge," said the buffalo. "What good would one of them do you?"

Again, Vecho begged piteously.

Vecho's crying and whining annoyed the buffalo to no end. He finally popped out an eye and gave it to Vecho.

Off Vecho went, with one tiny mouse eye and one huge buffalo eye. The mouse eye made everything appear a tenth its size. The buffalo eye made everything appear twice its size. Plus the mouse eye sloshed around, and the buffalo eye bulged and grew dry. Vecho wound up with a pounding headache. It took him a long time to get home.

"Vecho," said his wife. "Your eyes! One is tiny, one is huge." She furrowed her brow. "What on earth did you do now?"

Vecho told her how the day had gone.

His wife nodded. "Maybe it's time to stop trying to impress people. You don't have to be important. You don't have be amazing. Most of us aren't."

Vecho thought about that. "You're right."

TYPES OF TRANSPLANTS

Sometimes when a person is sick or injured and one of their organs fails—such as the liver, a lung, a kidney, the pancreas, or even the heart—surgeons can transplant a healthy organ from a donor. In this story, the mouse and the buffalo are organ donors; they give up an eyeball. But in reality, eyeballs cannot be transplanted. That's because the eye cannot do its job without the optic nerve, and so far modern medicine has not successfully transplanted the nerve along with the eyeball. However, the cornea of the eye, the clear outer layer that protects it from dirt and germs, can be transplanted. This is the most frequent type of transplant, restoring sight to people all around the globe.

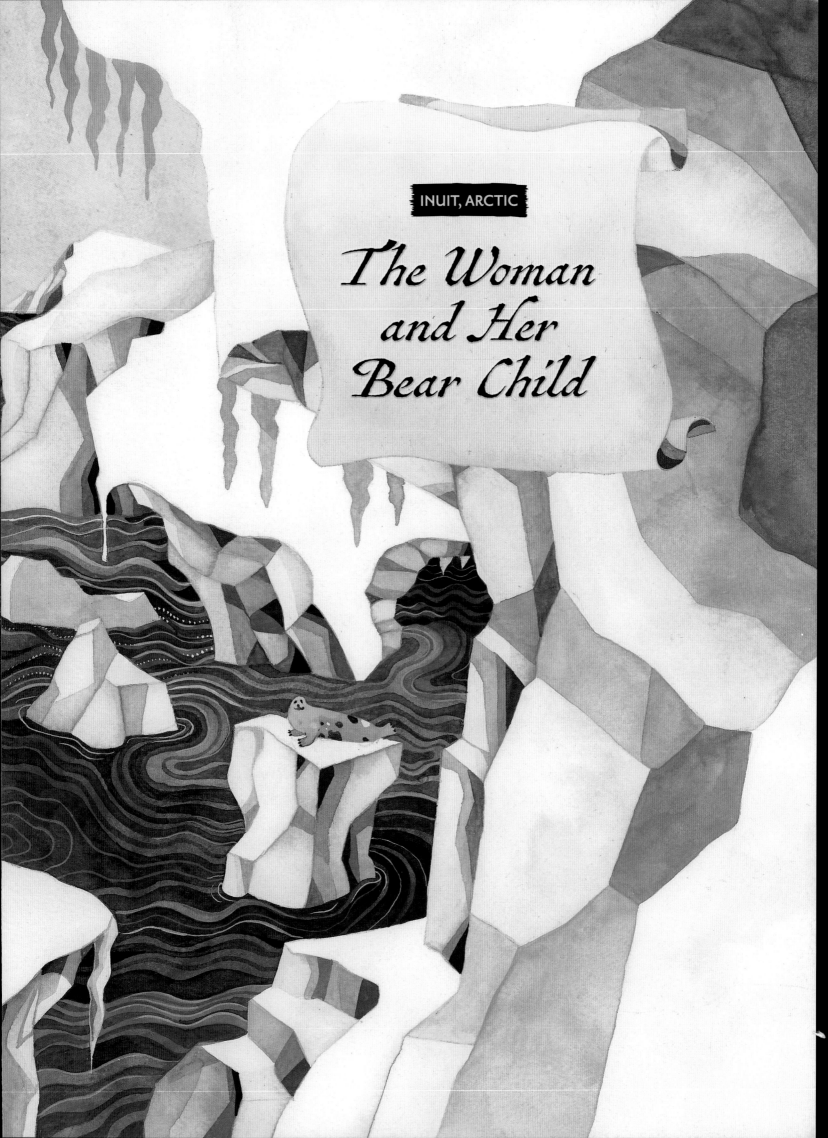

INUIT, ARCTIC

The Woman and Her Bear Child

A n old woman walked along the icy shore. The wind swept low and fast over the snow-covered land, hiding her tracks as quickly as she made them. Her whole body was covered with seal-skins, from her big hood all the way down to her boots, so her body wasn't cold. Yet inside, in her heart and soul, she felt frozen.

Men trudged past her, carrying three-pronged fishing spears and harpoons with walrus-tusk heads. They were husbands and sons of women she knew. They were on their way to hunt and fish, to feed their families. The old woman had no husband, no child. Her neighbors shared food with her, so her body wasn't hungry. But inside, in her heart and soul, she felt famished.

She stopped now and looked out to sea and let longing overtake her. If only she had a child to keep her heart and soul warm and nourished.

What was that? Out on a tip of ice? It was the size of an arctic hare, but the wrong shape. Was it a young fox? She walked closer. A polar bear cub sat there all alone. As the old woman approached, the cub cried. His tongue was bright pink under that shiny black nose.

The old woman walked closer still. The cub cried louder. He was tiny and pathetic. Why, he shouldn't have been out of his snow cave den yet. The woman turned in a circle, looking for the mamma bear. Any bear would have easily smelled her by now. That mamma bear should have come to her babe's rescue—she surely would have, if she could. She must be dead. Maybe this was the cub's first venture out into the world, to look for his mamma. The poor thing was lost. An orphan?

The old woman walked right up to the cub, who fixed his deep brown eyes on her. She picked him up and pressed her nose to his, in a traditional kiss, a *kunik*. The cub licked her nose in return. The old woman's heart and soul melted. "Hello, son," she said. "Hello, my darling Kunik." She held him to her chest, and he clung to her with his

baby arms and legs spread wide and his head tucked into her armpit.

Kunik ate and walked and slept with the old woman. Soon the village children took him rolling in the snow and sliding on the ice. Kunik was good at chasing snowballs and even at making them. In fact, he was the children's best playmate ever.

But Kunik didn't stay tiny for long. By spring, he was the size of a sled dog, and as independent and curious as any child. By autumn, he caught salmon for his old woman mother. By wintertime, he was even catching seals for her. It wasn't long before Kunik was the best fisher in the village.

Jealousy consumed the other hunters and fishers—they were being outshone by a bear! That was wrong. So the hunters and fishers hatched a plan to kill Kunik.

A little boy overheard the men and ran to tell the old woman. The

old woman threw her arms around Kunik and sobbed. This must not happen! She tramped from igloo to igloo, begging each hunter and fisher not to kill Kunik. "Kill me instead, please. Leave my sweet son alive."

"Hush, old woman. He's a big chunk of a bear already. The whole village can feast on him."

"Besides, bears are dangerous. It's amazing he hasn't realized already that we are prey. We can't have him hanging around."

The old woman hurried home to Kunik. "Run, my child, treasure of my heart and soul." She wiped away her tears as she spoke. "Run. Never return. Run, and live. But oh, do not go so far away that I cannot find you, for I must see you again. One day. Please."

Kunik loped away.

The old woman and the children sat quiet, blanketed in their sorrow.

Time passed, winter followed winter, and one day the old woman missed Kunik so much she simply had to see him. She walked along the icy tundra and called his name. She called and called. Finally, a huge bear came racing at her, fur shimmering white. Kunik and the old woman hugged each other. Kunik made a low, throaty moan. The old woman whispered, "I love you, too."

Kunik raced away as fast as he had come. He returned with a seal. The old woman cut it up and they enjoyed a blubbery meal together. "I'll be back tomorrow," said the old woman. "I promise."

They met every day, just like that. Kunik fed his old woman mother, and his old woman mother praised him and hugged him and gave him nose kisses. If you're lucky and you pay attention, you might see them out your window, warm and nourished in each other's love.

INUIT TRADITIONS
Inuit are a group of people who traditionally live in Arctic areas of Alaska, Canada, Greenland, and Siberia. These places offer mostly fish, fowl, and meat to eat, with some berries and plants in summer. Inuit make good use of the entire body of the animals they hunt. Muscles and organs make food; skins make clothing; blubber fuels lamps; and bones are carved and shaved for tools, household items, jewelry, and sculptures. Inuit respect and appreciate the animals they rely on for survival, including the massive and dangerous polar bear, holding in reverence the tight bond between mother bear and cub.

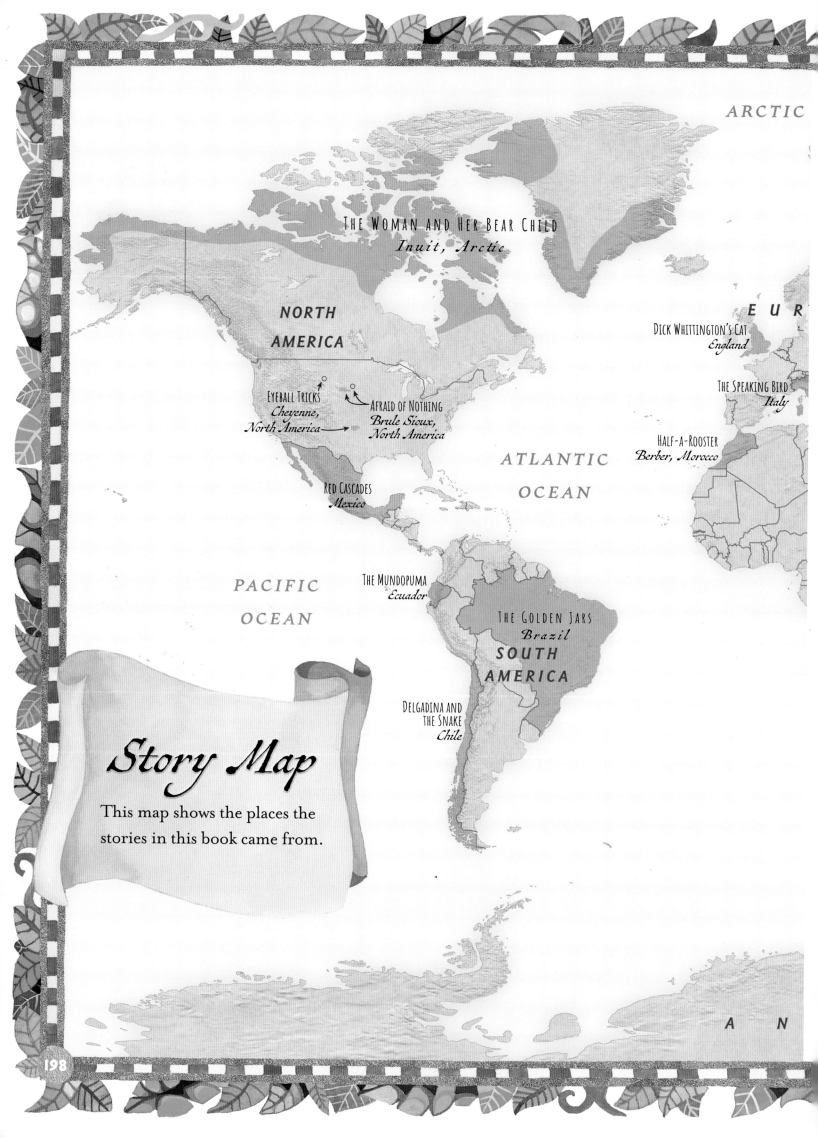

ARCTIC

THE WOMAN AND HER BEAR CHILD
Inuit, Arctic

NORTH
AMERICA

EUR

DICK WHITTINGTON'S CAT
England

EYEBALL TRICKS
*Cheyenne,
North America*

AFRAID OF NOTHING
*Brule Sioux,
North America*

THE SPEAKING BIRD
Italy

HALF-A-ROOSTER
Berber, Morocco

ATLANTIC

OCEAN

RED CASCADES
Mexico

PACIFIC

OCEAN

THE MUNDOPUMA
Ecuador

THE GOLDEN JARS
Brazil
SOUTH
AMERICA

DELGADINA AND
THE SNAKE
Chile

Story Map

This map shows the places the
stories in this book came from.

A N

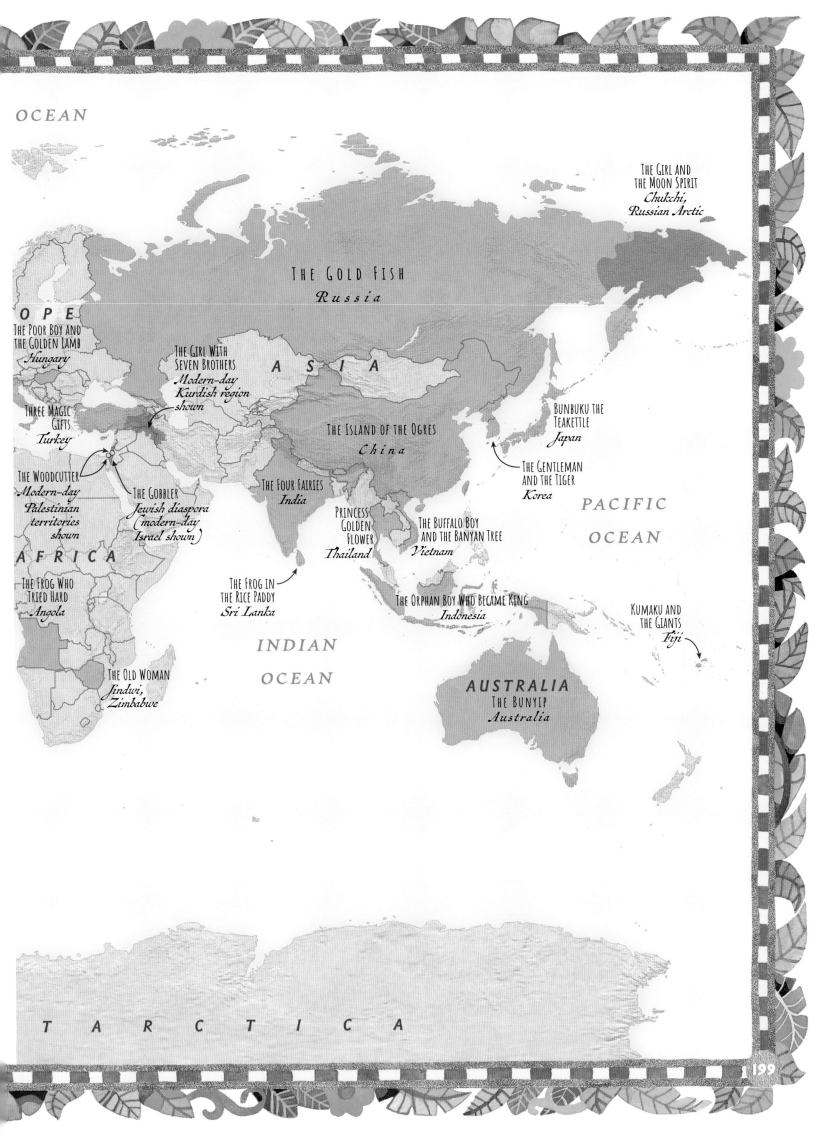

OCEAN

THE GIRL AND
THE MOON SPIRIT
*Chukchi,
Russian Arctic*

THE GOLD FISH
Russia

OPE

THE POOR BOY AND
THE GOLDEN LAMB
Hungary

THE GIRL WITH
SEVEN BROTHERS
*Modern-day
Kurdish region
shown*

ASIA

BUNBUKU THE
TEAKETTLE
Japan

THREE MAGIC
GIFTS
Turkey

THE ISLAND OF THE OGRES
China

THE GENTLEMAN
AND THE TIGER
Korea

THE WOODCUTTER
*Modern-day
Palestinian
territories
shown*

THE GOBBLER
*Jewish diaspora
(modern-day
Israel shown)*

THE FOUR FAIRIES
India

PACIFIC

OCEAN

AFRICA

PRINCESS
GOLDEN
FLOWER
Thailand

THE BUFFALO BOY
AND THE BANYAN TREE
Vietnam

THE FROG WHO
TRIED HARD
Angola

THE FROG IN
THE RICE PADDY
Sri Lanka

THE ORPHAN BOY WHO BECAME KING
Indonesia

KUMAKU AND
THE GIANTS
Fiji

INDIAN

OCEAN

THE OLD WOMAN
*Jindwi,
Zimbabwe*

AUSTRALIA
THE BUNYIP
Australia

TARCTICA

When I gathered these magical tales, I had several goals. The first was to make the reader laugh, something so needed today. So I couldn't pass up a story about a braggart whose desire to be amazing nearly ruins him and whose wife points out that most of us aren't amazing. And I snatched up a story about a man who's not afraid of ghosts but is terrified of a spider that a little girl plucks off him. Cleverness and total lack of smarts both bring laughs.

Some of these tales, however, don't have humorous plots, yet they appealed to my funny bone. This is where I found myself as a writer in new territory. I have often retold myths and religious stories, and I tend to be reverential in tone. But these magical tales are tradition, not religion. Delivering tradition to the modern child calls for making the stories palatable, memorable, hopefully delightful. So I retold them with the modern sensibility in mind, seeking to expose humor in the ways people converse and reflect upon their own situations.

My next goal was to find a variety of magic types. These stories present talking animals, of course, but also a stick that will smack people if ordered to. We find familiar magic—a turban that makes the wearer invisible—but also unexpected magic: a woman's knee that can hold inside it her children and their dogs. But, importantly, over and over we see that magic is limited. The denizens of the knee can come out into the world at will, but when someone throws a cloth over the woman, the children can't manage to get past the cloth and into the knee again. Magic has to be limited, or those with the magic would always win and the stories wouldn't be interesting.

And I included stories that challenge ideas of what constitutes magic. In one, a prince believes he's a turkey. Where's the magic? Well, who's to say whether he is or isn't? To what extent can our psychological state carry us into realities implausible to others? And there's a story about an old woman who adopts a polar bear cub, which then must run away before the villagers kill him. But the woman and the now adult bear meet regularly to share food. Magic? Is overcoming instincts to flee in fear and to hunt down prey magic? Is love magic?

I also wanted stories to transport the reader to different times and places. My goal was not to be representative but simply to offer a sampling. We start out bumping around Europe, then hop south to three countries in Africa. We move to places in the eastern Mediterranean, then head to northern Asia and around East Asia. We circle westward into India and Sri Lanka, then head east again, stopping along the way, to Australia. We cross the Pacific via Fiji, then on to South America and north into Central America and North America. It's a floppy global loop, with preference for indigenous stories over colonialist stories.

Finally, I wanted to tell stories my readers probably didn't know unless they came from the place of a given story. I originally expected these stories to differ from one another in themes. But once I had the final collection together, I saw persistent themes from all over.

Repeatedly, we meet single parents and young orphans. In the early Middle Ages, a lucky person might live into her 60s. But in the 1300s, bubonic plague devastated Africa, Asia, and Europe—life expectancy fell to 45. A short life expectancy persisted for the next few hundred years. Thus, it seems inevitable that in these tales the specter of death is ever present.

That specter is sometimes clothed in glory, however. A poor boy who happens upon a banyan tree with leaves that can revive the dead winds up hanging on to the tree's roots as it flies to the moon. That's where he stays. Lonely. But he looks down at his parents' faces for consolation. An orphan has astonishing luck, only to find that the source of it is a girl who lives in the sun. They love each other, but all the boy can do is look up at her in the sky and say the word that made her fall in love with him.

We also meet hungry people and homeless people. Children are sent to work because families can't feed them—and they are luckier than the child who has to sleep wherever he can because he has no family. We meet adults who have nothing more to eat than the powder left in the bottom of the mortar after grinding rice for the wealthy employer.

But the characters in these tales do not find "the answer to life" in wealth. While some dream about luxury, those dreams are held up as deceptive. A mangled rooster has the opportunity to marry a queen, but he realizes that he doesn't even know her and he'd rather go back to his own life, just without the interference of a cruel person there. A frog manages to do a king's bidding, for which he is to receive treasures. But those biddings make him deal with treachery and mortal danger. In the end he returns to his simple life in the rice paddy. Wealth simply doesn't bring happiness nor even make life more bearable.

Yet life is bearable; most characters in these tales do not behave like desperate people. Rather, they are resilient and resourceful. They

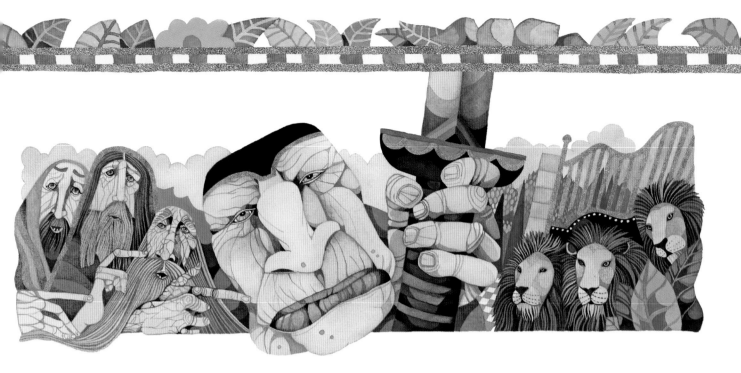

enjoy playing the flute for the sheep they herd all day. They befriend the ogres that surround them. When they are turned into swans, they maintain their habits of laughing, singing, and telling jokes. Indeed, laughter and music are keys, even to survival itself. A princess will die if she doesn't laugh—and a simple shepherd saves her. A whole people are threatened by a jaguar, who gets lured into a trap by the power of music, and thus all are saved.

And in these tales we find acts of kindness. An orphan grows up, earns money, and builds a church, a hospital, and a public bathroom. A passing gentleman picks up hitchhikers, then gets them to act as a team to save a girl from a tiger. A girl bandages a bird's broken wing and frees a rabbit from brambles and brings a tethered cow fresh water. Another girl takes in a brutal stepmother. None of these acts is done with the intention of a reward; it's simply kindness.

Imagine people coming together to listen to stories so many years ago. What could be better than a storyteller whose voice is melodic as music, carrying us into the magic? What could be better than laughing at the foibles and cleverness of the characters? What could make us want to come back the next night for additional stories more than the reassurance that, with resilience, resourcefulness, and kindness, we can make decent lives? I should have expected these themes. I hope their power helps readers find reassurance in these difficult times.

Bibliography

The versions of the stories in this book are often only very loosely based on the listed sources.

The Speaking Bird

Thompson, Stith. "The Dancing Water, the Singing Apple, and the Speaking Bird." In *One Hundred Favorite Folktales*, 319-325. Bloomington, IN: Indiana University Press, 1968.

Freeman, Benjamin G., and Graham A. Montgomery. "Using Song Playback Experiments to Measure Species Recognition Between Geographically Isolated Populations: A Comparison With Acoustic Trait Analyses." *The Auk: Ornithological Advances* 134.4 (2017): 857-870.

Dick Whittington's Cat

Smith, Niz, and Avril Lethbridge. "Dick Whittington and His Cat. An English Story Retold." n.d. worldstories.org.uk/reader/dick-whittington-and-his-cat/english/244.

McCormick, Michael. "Rats, Communications, and Plague: Toward an Ecological History." *Journal of Interdisciplinary History* 34.1 (2003): 1-25.

The Poor Boy and the Golden Lamb

Thompson, Stith. "The Lamb With the Golden Fleece." In *One Hundred Favorite Folktales*, 265-266. Bloomington, IN: Indiana University Press, 1968.

Felföldi, László. 2001. "Connections Between Dance and Dance Music: Summary of Hungarian Research." *Yearbook for Traditional Music* 33 (2001): 159-166.

Half-a-Rooster

Scheub, Harold (compiler). "Half-a-Cock." In *African Tales*, 48-51. Madison, WI: University of Wisconsin Press, 2005.

Foltz, Richard C. *Animals in Islamic Traditions and Muslim Cultures*. London: Oneworld Publications, 2014.

The Frog Who Tried Hard

Chatelain, Héli, ed. "The Son of Kimanaueze and the Daughter of Sun and Moon." In *Folk-tales of Angola*, 131-140. Boston/New York: Houghton Mifflin, 1894. library.si.edu/digital-library/book/folktalesofango00chat.

W. W. N. "Folk-tales of Angola: The Daughter of Lord Sun and Lady Moon." *The Journal of American Folklore* 7.24 (1894): 61-65.

jstor.org/stable/532961?seq=1#metadata_info_tab_contents.

Shepard, Aaron. "How Frog Went to Heaven." *School Magazine* (July 1996). aaronshep.com/stories/044.html.

Giesa, Tristan, Melis Arslan, Nicola M. Pugno, and Markus J. Buehler. "Nanoconfinement of Spider Silk Fibrils Begets Superior Strength, Extensibility, and Toughness." *Nano Letters* 11.11 (2011): 5038-5046.

Griffiths, J. R., and V. R. Salanitri. "The Strength of Spider Silk." *Journal of Materials Science* 15.2 (1980): 491-496.

The Old Woman

Scheub, Harold (compiler). "The Old Woman." In *African Tales*, 98-101. Madison, WI: University of Wisconsin Press, 2005.

García-Lara, Silverio, and Sergio O. Serna-Saldivar. "Corn History and Culture." In *Corn: Chemistry and Technology*, 3rd ed., 1-18. Woodhead Publishing and AACC International Press, 2019.

The Woodcutter

Muhawi, Ibrahim, and Sharif Kanaana. "The Woodcutter." In *Speak, Bird, Speak Again: Palestinian Arab Folktales*, 267-271. Berkeley, CA: University of California Press, 1989.

El-Zein, Amira. *Islam, Arabs, and Intelligent World of the Jinn*. Syracuse, NY: Syracuse University Press, 2009.

The Girl With Seven Brothers

Edgecomb, Diane. "A Sister With Seven Brothers." In *A Fire in My Heart: Kurdish Tales*, 88-91. Westport, CT/London: Libraries Unlimited, 2008. This story was collected by Yuksel Serindag in 2007. Additional parts were added by Saadat Fidan in 2007.

Foltz, Richard. "The 'Original' Kurdish Religion? Kurdish Nationalism and the False Conflation of the Yezidi and Zoroastrian Traditions." *Journal of Persianate Studies* 10.1 (2017): 87-106.

Izady, Mehrdad R. *The Kurds: A Concise Handbook*, 137-138. Taylor and Francis, 1992.

Three Magic Gifts

Kúnos, Ignácz (writer), and Willy Pogány (illustrator). "The Magic Turban, the Magic Whip and the Magic Carpet." In *Forty-Four Turkish Fairy Tales*, 87-94. London: George G. Harrap and Co., 1913.

Hosseini, Arezou. "Iran's Sherbet and Sherbet Houses in Passage of Time." *Bagh-e Nazar* 10. 25 (2013): 49-58.

The Gobbler

Gordon, Yossy. "The Turkey Prince." 2007. Attributed to Rabbi Nachman of Breslov. chabad.org/library/article_cdo/aid/612171/jewish/The-Turkey-Prince.htm.

Heller, Joshua, Rabbi. "The Kosher Turkey Debate." n.d. myjewishlearning.com/article/traditions-and-counter-traditions.

Regenstein, Joe M., and Muhammad Chaudry. "A Brief Introduction to Some of the Practical Aspects of the Kosher and Halal Laws for the Poultry Industry." In *Poultry Meat Processing*, eds. C. M. Owens, C. Z. Alvarado, and A. R. Sams, 281. London: CRC Press, 2001.

The Gold Fish

Thompson, Stith. "The Goldfish." In *One Hundred Favorite Folktales*, 241-243. Bloomington, IN: Indiana University Press, 1968.

Hilton, Alison. *Russian Folk Art*. Bloomington, IN: Indiana University Press, 1995.

The Girl and the Moon Spirit

Marshall, Bonnie C. (translator and reteller) and Kira van Deusen (ed.). "The Girl and the Moon Spirit." In *Far North Tales: Stories From the Peoples of the Arctic Circle*, 162-164. Santa Barbara, CA/Denver, CO/Oxford, U.K.: Libraries Unlimited, 2011.

MacDonald, John. *The Arctic Sky: Inuit Astronomy, Star Lore, and Legend*. Toronto: Royal Ontario Museum, 1998.

The Gentleman and the Tiger

In-Sob, Zong. "The Young Gentleman and the Tiger." In *Folk Tales From Korea*. New York: Greenwood Press Publishers, 1969.

Winter, Steve, and Sharon Guynup. *Tigers Forever: Saving the World's Most Endangered Big Cat*. Washington, DC: National Geographic, 2013.

Bunbuku the Teakettle

Freeman-Mitford, Algernon Bertram. "The Accomplished and Lucky Teakettle." In *Tales of Old Japan*, 252-254. London: Macmillan and Co., 1871.

Mayer, Fanny Hagin, ed. *Ancient Tales in Modern Japan: An Anthology of Japanese Folk Tales*. Bloomington, IN: Indiana University Press, 1985.

Brazil, Mark, and Masayuki Yabuuchi. *A Pocket Guide to the Common and Iconic Mammals of Japan*. Japan Nature Guides. Notsuke-gun, Hokkaido, Japan, 2015.

Saeki, Midori. "Ecology and Conservation of the Raccoon Dog (*Nyctereutes procyonoides*) in Japan." Dissertation, University of Oxford, 2001.

Tanaka, Hiroshi. "Seasonal and Daily Activity Patterns of Japanese Badgers (*Meles meles anakuma*) in Western Honshu, Japan." *Mammal Study* 30.1 (2005): 11-17.

The Island of the Ogres

Wilhelm, Richard, ed. "The Kingdom of the Ogres." In *The Chinese Fairy Book*, 189-196. Translated after original sources by Frederick H. Martens. New York: Frederick A. Stokes Company, 1921.

Deng, Gang, and Teng Kang. *Chinese Maritime Activities and Socioeconomic Development, C. 2100 BC-1900 AD*. No. 188. Westport, CT: Greenwood Publishing Group, 1997.

Wiens, Herold J. "Riverine and Coastal Junks in China's Commerce." *Economic Geography* 31.3 (1955): 248-264.

The Four Fairies

Teverson, Andrew, ed. *The Fairy Tale World*, 316. London: Routledge, 2019.

Bayly, Christopher A. "The Origins of Swadeshi (Home Industry): Cloth and Indian Society." In *The Social Life of Things: Commodities in Cultural Perspective*, ed. A. Apadurai, 285-321. Cambridge, U.K.: Cambridge University Press, 1986.

The Frog in the Rice Paddy

Parker, H. "The Frog Prince (A Tale From Sri Lanka)." In *Village Folk Tales of Ceylon*, vol. 1. London: Luzac and Company, 1910.

Khatiwada, Janak Raj, Subarna Ghimire, Shanta Paudel Khatiwada, Bikash Paudel, Richard Bischof, Jianping Jiang, and Torbjørn Haugaasen. "Frogs as Potential Biological Control Agents in the Rice Fields of Chitwan, Nepal." *Agriculture, Ecosystems & Environment* 230 (2016): 307-314.

Princess Golden Flower

Toth, Marian Davies. "Phikool Thong." In *Tales From Thailand*, 66-72. Rutland, VT/Tokyo: Charles E. Tuttle Company, 1971.

Goody, Jack. *The Culture of Flowers*. Cambridge, U.K.: Cambridge University Press, 1993.

The Buffalo Boy and the Banyan Tree

Schultz, George F. "The Buffalo Boy and the Banyan Tree." In *Vietnamese Legends*, 31-33. Rutland, VT/Tokyo: Charles E. Tuttle Company, 1965.

Vatikiotis, Michael R. J. *Political Change in South-East Asia: Trimming the Banyan Tree*. Abingdon, U.K.: Routledge, 2005.

The Orphan Boy Who Became King

Knappert, Jan. "How the Orphan Boy Became King." In *Myths and Legends of Indonesia*, 191-192. Singapore/Kuala Lumpur/Hong Kong: Heinemann Educational Books (Asia) Ltd., 1977.

Suryadinata, Leo, Evi Nurvidya Arifin, and Aris Ananta. *Indonesia's Population: Ethnicity and Religion in a Changing Political Landscape*. Singapore: Institute of Southeast Asian Studies, 2003.

The Bunyip

Lang, Andrew, ed. "The Bunyip." In *The Brown Fairy Book*, 71-76. New York: Dover Publications, Inc., 1965.

Menkhorst, Peter, Danny Rodgers, Rohan Clarke, Jeff Davies, Peter Marsack, and Kim Franklin. *The Australian Bird Guide*. Princeton, NJ: Princeton University Press, 2017.

Kumaku and the Giants

Reed, A. W., and Inez Hames. "Kumaku and the Giant." *Myths and Legends of Fiji and Rotuma*, 133-137. Wellington/Auckland/Sydney: Reed, 1967.

Worthy, Trevor H., and Atholl Anderson. "Results of Palaeofaunal Research." In *The Early Prehistory of Fiji*, eds. G. Clark and A. Anderson, 41-62. Canberra, Australia: ANU Press, 2009.

Field, Michael. "Fiji Revealed as Land of Lost Giants, Including Huge Chicken." 1999. www.pireport.org/articles/1999/07/30/fiji-revealed-land-lost-giants-including-huge-chicken.

The Mundopuma

Uzendoski, Michael A., and Edith Felicia Calapucha-Tapuy. "The Mundopuma Story Told by Anibal Andy (El Ductur) During an Open-Mike Storytelling Contest." In *The Ecology of the Spoken Word: Amazonian Storytelling and Shamanism Among the Napo Runa*, 150-155. Urbana, Chicago, and Springfield, IL: University of Illinois Press, 2012.

Benson, Elizabeth P. "The Lord, the Ruler: Jaguar Symbolism in the Americas." In *Icons of Power: Feline Symbolism in the Americas*, ed. N. J. Saunders, 53-76. London/New York: Routledge, 1998.

Mendoza, Miguel Saavedra, Paúl Cun, Eric Horstman, Sonia Carabajo, and Juan José Alava. "The Last Coastal Jaguars of Ecuador: Ecology, Conservation and Management Implications." In *Big Cats*. IntechOpen, 2017. intechopen.com/books/big-cats/the-last-coastal-jaguars-of-ecuador-ecology-conservation-and-management-implications.

The Golden Jars

de Almeida, Livia, and Ana Portella. "The Golden Jars." In *Brazilian Folktales*, 75-77. Westport, CT/London: Libraries Unlimited, 2006.

Andrade, Denis V., Otavio A. Marques, Rodrigo S. Gavira, Fausto E. Barbo, Rogério L. Zacariotti, and Ivan Sazima. "Tail Luring by the Golden Lancehead (*Bothrops insularis*), an Island Endemic Snake From South-Eastern Brazil." *South American Journal of Herpetology* 5.3 (2010): 175-180.

Lucas, Sylvia. "Spiders in Brazil." *Toxicon* 26.9 (1988): 759-772.

Ribeiro, Luiz F., Marcos R. Bornschein, Ricardo Belmonte-Lopes, Carina R. Firkowski, Sergio A. A. Morato, and Marcio R. Pie. "Seven New Microendemic Species of *Brachycephalus* (Anura: Brachycephalidae) From Southern Brazil." *PeerJ* 3 (2015): e1011.

Delgadina and the Snake

Pino-Saavedra, Yolando, ed. "Delgadina and the Snake." In *Folktales of Chile*, 72-77. Translated by Rockwell Gray. Chicago: University of Chicago Press, 1967.

Lillywhite, Harvey B. *How Snakes Work*. Oxford, U.K.: Oxford University Press, 2014.

Red Cascades

Vigil, Angel. "The Waterfall of Wisdom." In *The Eagle on the Cactus: Traditional Stories From Mexico*, 124-126. Translated by Francisco Miraval. Englewood, CO: Libraries Unlimited, Inc., 2000.

McKeever Furst, Jill Leslie. *The Natural History of the Soul in Ancient Mexico*. New Haven, CT: Yale University Press, 1997.

Afraid of Nothing

Erdoes, Richard, and Alfonso Ortiz, eds. "The Man Who Was Afraid of Nothing." In *American Indian Myths and Legends*, 435-438. New York: Pantheon Books, 1984. Told by Lame Deer, and recorded by Richard Erdoes.

Brodie, Edmund D. "Toxins and Venoms." *Current Biology* 19.20 (2009): R931-R935.

Eyeball Tricks

Erdoes, Richard, and Alfonso Ortiz, eds. "Doing a Trick With Eyeballs." In *American Indian Myths and Legends*, 379-381. New York: Pantheon Books, 1984. Told by Rachel Strange Owl in Birney, Montana, in 1971, and recorded by Richard Erdoes.

Gain, Philippe, Rémy Jullienne, Zhiguo He, Mansour Aldossary, Sophie Acquart, Fabrice Cognasse, and Gilles Thuret. "Global Survey of Corneal Transplantation and Eye Banking." *JAMA Ophthalmology* 134.2 (2016): 167-173.

The Woman and Her Bear Child

Friedman, Amy. 1997. "The Woman and Her Bear." *Oklahoman* (January 20, 1997). Accessed on April 3, 2021: oklahoman.com/article/2567308/the-woman-and-her-bear.

Freeman, Milton, and Lee Foote, eds. *Inuit, Polar Bears, and Sustainable Use: Local, National and International Perspectives*. Alberta, Canada: CCI Press of the University of Alberta, 2009. Accessed April 7, 2020. uap.ualberta.ca/book-images/Open%20Access/9781772121902_WEB.pdf#page=150.

Index

Boldface indicates illustration; **boldface** page spans include text and illustrations.

For Dr. Michael Link and Dr. Colin Driscoll of the Mayo Clinic,
for performing the best magic ever. — *DJN*

For my beautiful granddaughter Pris Noah Lines Croucher, born whilst I
was painting this book. I can't wait to read these stories out loud to her ...
when she's a little bigger. — *CB*

✯

Since 1888, the National Geographic Society has
funded more than 14,000 research, conservation,
education, and storytelling projects around the world.
National Geographic Partners distributes a portion of
the funds it receives from your purchase to National
Geographic Society to support programs including the
conservation of animals and their habitats. To learn
more, visit natgeo.com/info.

For more information, visit nationalgeographic.com,
call 1-877-873-6846, or write to the following address:

National Geographic Partners, LLC
1145 17th Street N.W.
Washington, DC 20036-4688 U.S.A.

For librarians and teachers: nationalgeographic.com/
books/librarians-and-educators

More for kids from National Geographic:
natgeokids.com

National Geographic Kids magazine inspires children to
explore their world with fun yet educational articles
on animals, science, nature, and more. Using fresh
storytelling and amazing photography, *Nat Geo Kids*
shows kids ages 6 to 14 the fascinating truth about
the world—and why they should care.
kids.nationalgeographic.com/subscribe

For rights or permissions inquiries, please contact
National Geographic Books Subsidiary Rights:
bookrights@natgeo.com

Designed by Callie Broaddus

The publisher thanks researcher Michelle Harris and
cultural sensitivity reviewer Ebonye Gussine Wilkins
for their invaluable assistance with this book. Thanks
also to Dr. Anton Treuer, Professor of Ojibwe at
Bemidji State University.

Hardcover ISBN: 978-1-4263-7248-3
Reinforced library binding ISBN:
978-1-4263-7249-0

Printed in Hong Kong
21/PPHK/1

✯

All Illustrations by Christina Balit

Sidebar background (throughout), Naoki Kim/Adobe Stock; 17, michaklootwijk/Adobe Stock; 21, Peter Smith/Alamy
Stock Photo; 28, Andocs/Shutterstock; 35 (LO), Phuong D. Nguyen/Shutterstock; 41, papkin/Shutterstock; 47, Gideon
Mendel/Getty Images; 57, Byelikova Oksana/Adobe Stock; 61, Martin Gray/National Geographic Image Collection;
72, mirzamlk/Shutterstock; 79, Randy Rimland/Shutterstock; 83, Juriaan Wossink/Alamy Stock Photo; 90, an-Stefan
Knick/EyeEm/Getty Images; 96, Vladimir Medvedev/Nature Picture Library; 103, 23frogger/Shutterstock; 110, Media-
Production/Getty Images; 116, Tuul & Bruno Morandi/Getty Images; 123, photolife95/Adobe Stock; 128, giemgiem/
Adobe Stock; 135, huythoai/Adobe Stock; 138, Edmund Lowe Photography/Shutterstock; 147 (UP), Ivan/Adobe Stock; 151
(LO), RichLindie/Getty Images; 158, Melissa Groo/National Geographic Image Collection; 167, reptiles4all/Getty Images;
173, llukee/Alamy Stock Photo; 178, DEA/G. Dagli Orti/De Agostini via Getty Images; 185 (UP), Marek Velechovsky/
Shutterstock; 191 (LO), bluecinema/Getty Images; 197, Cristina Mittermeier/National Geographic Image Collection